39 BERNE STREET

GLOBAL AFRICAN VOICES
Dominic Thomas, editor

39
BERNE STREET

MAX LOBE

Translated by Johanna McCalmont

INDIANA UNIVERSITY PRESS

This book is a publication of

Indiana University Press
Office of Scholarly Publishing
Herman B Wells Library 350
1320 East 10th Street
Bloomington, Indiana 47405 USA

iupress.org

Originally published as *39 rue de Berne* by Max Lobe © Editions Zoe, 2013. Published by arrangement with Agence lltteraire Astier-Pacher.

Manufactured in the United States of America

First printing 2023

Cataloging information is available from the Library of Congress.

ISBN 978-0-253-06492-9 (paperback)
ISBN 978-0-253-06493-6 (ebook)

To my mother, Chandèze.

39 BERNE STREET

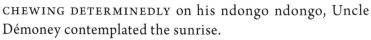

CHEWING DETERMINEDLY on his ndongo ndongo, Uncle Démoney contemplated the sunrise.

It was more than a routine for him. It was an essential daily ritual. A religion.

His ndongo ndongo, a thirty-centimeter rattan stem as thick as a cigar, served as a toothbrush. My uncle simply had no desire to buy himself a regular one. That's what we use over here, he would say, a well-dried-out ndongo ndongo.

I don't know why Uncle Démoney spent so much time on oral hygiene. As a child, I used to think it was some sort of ablution he performed before communing with his sun god during his morning prayers. I was even convinced that God never answered prayers from foul-smelling mouths.

The sun god hadn't risen yet, but Uncle Démoney was already emerging from his hut, lumbering like an old elephant. He didn't really look like a big old elephant with dangerous tusks, though; he was pretty skinny.

That morning, outside his dilapidated little house, Démoney yawned and raised his hands. He had tied a long, faded, multicolored loincloth tight around his waist. He rubbed his sunken eyes with his dry hands. The fine lines on his face stood out, even though he was still young, barely fifty years old. With one hand, he shaded his eyes and looked up at the sky in search of his sun god who was yet to appear. He smiled.

Still chewing hard on his ndongo ndongo, Démoney began to clean his teeth. He loved to say it was the only thing left for him to do in a country where people listed unemployment as a skill. In Ngodi-Akwa, my uncle had been one of the lucky few to have ever had a job. Now he was like everyone else, a jobless hustler.

Any time we spent our holidays in Cameroon, my mother, Mbila, refused point-blank to sleep in the Ngodi-Akwa marshland where her brother lived, a brother she respectfully called Papa. She always stayed in a hotel with several stars in downtown Douala. But I always really wanted to see my uncle, so she'd leave me with him and come back for me a few days later. That's how I ended up talking to her about what he did when he woke up.

"Mama, there's something I want to ask you," I said. "Why does Uncle Démoney always get up early-early in the morning, when everyone else in the neighborhood is still sleeping?"

"Because other people don't have anything to do. They don't have any work."

"But Uncle Démoney doesn't have any work either."

"Yes, that's right. But your uncle has stuck to his old routine. He still acts like he has a job. So, you see, that's why he gets up early-early every morning."

I realized that when Uncle got up early now, instead of putting on the black trousers Auntie Bilolo had pressed with the charcoal iron and going to work, he settled for his old multicolored loincloth and watching the sunrise. Anyway, don't they say the early bird catches the worm?

There had been a time when Uncle Démoney was a tax inspector. And believe you me, that was no mean feat! To become a tax inspector, you had to be appointed directly by the political authorities: assistant divisional officers, divisional officers, mayors, governors, and even the president of the republic himself.

So it was the assistant divisional officers, divisional officers, mayors, governors, and even the president of the republic who had elevated Uncle Démoney by appointing him tax inspector.

But as my uncle said, "It's the ones who raise you up who eventually bring you back down, right down, in fact." Which was exactly what happened to him. Now Uncle Démoney was just a fallen, withered old man.

At my uncle's house, people always talked about the political and administrative authorities, and above all the president of the republic, with a kind of fear that made me wonder. They were extremely suspicious and didn't say just any old thing about the president, oh no! It felt like Biya was everywhere. If he wasn't on the national TV station (which was new back then), his face showed up on every roadside. His image fought for space alongside all kinds of billboards. There were posters where President Biya always appeared young and smiling, posters declaring *Paul Biya, the man for the job*; *Paul Biya, the incarnation of austerity*; *Paul Biya, the people's call*; *Paul Biya, for Greater Ambitions for Cameroon*; and even *Paul Biya, the people's choice*. Any time anyone mentioned him, I thought he was nearby, watching us, listening to us even, and that he'd appear if we said anything bad about him. That's why I always spoke highly of His Excellency the president of the republic. But since I didn't actually have anything to say about him, I just kept quiet.

Despite his general wariness, Uncle Démoney acted tough and played the rebel. He was very angry with the president and what he called the regime. He'd say, "The regime is corrupt as shit." And he'd say it loud and clear to anyone who would listen.

That morning, my uncle carefully inspected the small drainage ditch below the veranda. He had dug it out and cemented it with his own hands, and it was now almost full to the brim with mud.

He had quickly made the drain to divert the turbid flow of water from the heavy July rains that streamed down into his marshland from the higher ground in the neighborhood. It was the only thing he could do to protect his hut.

Uncle had built his shack quick-quick. Auntie Bilolo, his wife, often reminded him that the building did not comply with local planning regulations. She said that might have been one reason why the political and administrative authorities who had elevated him had eventually brought him back down. Auntie Bilolo even went as far as predicting that they would be moved out by a bulldozer one day. Thankfully, that hadn't happened yet. But how much longer did they have?

Each time his wife uttered such threats, my uncle would send her back to her pots. "Since when do women know anything about local planning regulations? Planning regulations, political authorities, planning regulations, these authorities, those authorities—what do you know about all that? You can't even read your own name! Just go away and worry about what you've got cooking in your pots and pans!"

The moment arrived—the sun finally rose. A precious moment not to be missed. The first rays from Uncle's sun god lit up his aging face. He watched carefully, attentively, as the first light appeared in the clear sky. He seemed totally enraptured by this magic that no longer delighted anyone else. Not even the birds cared. He stopped rubbing his teeth and gums with the long ndongo ndongo, which he also used to whip his son, Pitou, who could be extremely stubborn.

Uncle Démoney was savoring this exquisite joy when all of a sudden, a rooster ruined the magic. The puny little creature wandered over, strutting his stuff like a nanga boko, like a drunken gigolo. He lazily fluttered this way and that before attempting to perch on the barbed wire protecting my uncle's hut.

To be honest, I'd always wondered what that fence was for—there was nothing to steal in Démoney's house. The parlor was a kind of ghost room with a small table, old-old from when Uncle had been someone. The faux-leather armchair and two wooden benches eaten away by humidity looked lost in the otherwise empty space.

Unlike my uncle, the sassy rooster was late. He took the liberty of sleeping in, even though it was his job to wake everyone early-early with a loud cock-a-doodle-doo. Uncle shooed him away with the back of his hand. It really wasn't the right time to disturb my uncle. The rooster ignored the threat. His flapping wings seemed to say to Uncle Démoney, "Yeah, I know I'm late; so what? Better late than never, so just let me get on with it and leave me in peace." Without further ado, the creature pulled itself up and began its chorus. My uncle was so angry he took a stone from under the muddy veranda and threw it right into the insolent bird's mouth. "Clear off! Dirty thing!" he cried. The rooster fled, fearing for its life.

Staring at the sun, Uncle began to mutter, but I couldn't hear a thing because I was so far away. I was hiding behind Auntie Bilolo's outdoor kitchen. That's where he banished her whenever she said anything he thought was stupid, especially if it involved bulldozers.

I took refuge back there. I knew that even if Uncle looked around outside his hut, he'd never deign to give this corner a crumb of his attention—it was women's business.

I wouldn't have understood what he was telling the sun anyway because he was speaking Bassa. Uncle Démoney talked to it like a son to his father. He shared his secrets. He whispered the way you would to an old friend. I don't know whether his sun god ever replied. But even if the sun remained mute, Uncle spoke to it. That day, to my great surprise, he began to cry. What?

Uncle was crying? Impossible! Anyone else could cry, but not him. What was he talking to his god about that made him cry? He had always told me, "My son, never let yourself be carried away by the white man's ways. He cries like a woman. And when he's not crying like a woman, he's off doing naughty things with another man."

Later, oh yes, many years later, I understood that those moments contemplating the sun offered him a glimmer of hope. Uncle Démoney sought hope in a country where dreaming of a better life was shameful, sinful almost. "In the past," Uncle would say wistfully, "you could study and hope to put it to use one day. Now, there's nothing! You're condemned to live in poverty forever and accept it, swallow it, keep it in your belly like medicine that's hard to take."

That same weakness and sense of annihilation is what I'm feeling this morning, locked up in my cell at Champ-Dollon Prison in Geneva. I wake early-early to watch the sunrise like my uncle used to. I cry the way my uncle didn't want me to. Contrary to what he wanted, I have become *like that*, like those white men he told me about.

EVEN IF UNCLE seemed to have been defeated by life in general, he hadn't lost his rebellious spirit by any means. Whenever he criticized the regime loudly, Auntie Bilolo would tell him to pull a pair of panty-drawers over his mouth. But he would say he'd talk if he wanted to. He had no desire to shut up. He'd even say he was going to change the world. As far as I know, Uncle had picked up his rebel habits from his father, Pa Ndoumbè. But that's how Pa Ndoumbè had gotten himself killed, joining the maquis against the colonizers. Uncle hadn't been very lucky. His mother, Ma Antoinette, had passed away a few days later, killed by a bite from a nasty bush snake. So Uncle had had to take care of little Mbila, whom he treated like his daughter. All that remained of Pa Ndoumbè and Ma Antoinette was a black-and-white photo hung-hung on a wall in his hut. Oh, I almost forgot—Pa Ndoumbè's spirit was still around to torment her husband too, as Auntie Bilolo often said.

Pa Ndoumbè had joined the maquis against the nkana, the white people. Uncle Démoney was fighting the regime, but that wasn't the only thing. His blacklist was long: the postcolonial dictatorship, the single-party system, injustice, and a whole lot of other things I can't remember.

When I went back to Cameroon in the summer of 2000, my uncle had added what he called collateral enemies to his blacklist: devaluation of the CFA franc, heavily indebted poor countries, budget deficits, the International Monetary Fund, the World Bank, hogwash, waste, misery, corruption . . . Each time he uttered those words, it was with such force and such palpable, burning rage that it was best not to approach him in case you were hit by one of his outpourings.

When you have the character of a maquisard, like my uncle, you can't help but annoy the political authorities. Then they lock you up in prison or even finish you off. It's a wonder the politicians never threw my uncle in prison. They even raised him up. But I think it was a way to get him to pull some drawers over his mouth, because those politicians are full-full of ways to quiet roosters that make too much fuss. They flatter you, saying you're cotas, you're pals; it's a real-real coterie between you. Then, once you're as thick as thieves, the way you are with real cotas, that's it—they drop you.

Tax inspector! What a wonderful job! Well, that's what my uncle thought—it's not something I've ever considered becoming. And given I'm writing this from Champ-Dollon Prison, I don't think I could ever become a tax inspector. My long prison sentence has severely blotted my record. At any rate, Uncle said there were many benefits to the job and huge potential for personal enrichment.

Uncle told me Cameroon had seen the CFA franc devalued in the early nineties; the country's coffers were empty, and public debt skyrocketed. The state had been forced to bow to the World Bank and International Monetary Fund, going cap in hand like a paralytic asking for alms: "Abeg, abeg, help us."

During those tough-tough times, Uncle was the only person in Ngodi-Akwa who worked for the government. Everyone thought he had entered the court of the big bosses. The shopkeepers in the city were dodging taxes, and if Mr. Tax Inspector wanted, he could take his share and keep his mouth shut. The matter was settled! But Uncle never gave in—either you paid up and he left you in peace, or you didn't pay up and he caused trouble. And I mean big trouble, until you were in it right up to your neck, over your head even. For him, being a tax inspector meant the serious responsibility of ensuring the state coffers were replenished.

Uncle shared these battles like a glass of palm wine with a few friends, fellow underground resistance fighters. All day long, he listened to the radio with those Ngodi-Akwa guys. The antenna of the little radio set was always stretched right up, as if searching for stray airwaves. It quietly-quietly spat out high-pitched noises. At times the signal dropped, and it barely croaked. Uncle and his friends would get angry. They'd hit the radio as if they were smacking the rear end of a badly behaved child. They would try moving it. They didn't want to miss any of the news, even though it was always the same: bad.

I worried about my uncle and his comrades a lot. That's what they called each other: comrades. Comrade Démoney, Comrade Kissoko, Comrade Tara, Comrade, Comrade . . . One day, my uncle shouted, "Hey, Comrade Dipita, bring us some water!" I fetched it with a great sense of pride, honored to be raised up to their level.

Those skinny men seemed tormented by every sound that came out of that little radio. I thought they'd give themselves heart attacks. I was pretty worried because at school in Geneva, where I lived, they'd told us a lot about cardiovascular disease, infarctions, and all sorts of things like that. They told us a heart attack could be caused by high blood pressure. And our teacher said you had to call an ambulance immediately if someone had a heart attack. But my uncle said there wasn't a single ambulance left in Ngodi-Akwa. So I was really scared I wouldn't be able to do anything to save my comrades if something happened.

The journalists and commentators talked-talked, o! Sometimes they paused when they got to the obituaries. Contrary to what I thought, the obituaries didn't offer my comrades any respite. You never knew what bad news the radio would bring: the death of a beloved long-lost aunt? The uncle of the aunt of the cousin of the nephew of your wife? Your cousin's child?

Apart from the obituaries, the radio occasionally offered some real entertainment with Bikutsi or Makossa music. That's when my comrades relaxed a little, happily drinking matango, palm wine. But, of course, they continued to criticize the regime between choruses. When the journalists returned to the news, it all went quiet again. The newsreaders' voices were monotonous, but they spoke louder each time they uttered the name of His Excellency the president of the republic. And that's when the chance of someone having a heart attack increased.

Apart from letting themselves be tormented by bad news, my comrades filled the gaping holes in their jobless days by reading newspaper articles. The articles were mostly from the opposition papers they picked up here and there from newsstands downtown.

When one of my comrades came across an article he felt wasn't hard enough on the regime, he'd share it with the others. He'd read an extract aloud, pulling all sorts of faces, sneering. Once he had finished reading, my comrades would blow off steam, outraged, shouting things like, "Whoever wrote this article is a real-real spokesman for the regime! Only a journalist who has sold his soul to the devil could write something like that!"

When one of them, usually my uncle, came across an article that was suitably critical of the president and his regime, he'd read it loud and clear for his comrades. They would applaud and congratulate each other like they had just made a discovery worthy of a Nobel Prize. They'd even go as far as unanimously calling for the brave author of the article to be promoted. Between rounds of applause or outrage, my uncle would promise to share his thoughts with an opposition paper. "One day, one day," he'd say with conviction. He told himself he'd write a column to show biddable journalists how not to put the cap back on their ballpoint pens.

As for me, I didn't really understand much of what my noisy comrades said. Their debates were such a cacophony, so passionate, so wild you would have thought they were fighting over land or a woman. In Cameroon, they say football unites men, but problems with land or women are sure to divide.

Their discussions didn't always make me fret. Sometimes I laughed so hard I thought my sides would split when I saw the serious expressions on their faces. I thought they would make excellent actors. But I never laughed for long before their quarrels made me worry again. They'd get angry and would even be ready to fight.

"Oh! Comrade Démoney, forget all that! You just act tough; you're just a coward, a mougou," Comrade Tara once shouted.

"A mougou? Me? Not quite right in the head, are you, Tara? Wash that insult out of your mouth now-now!"

"Yes, you, Démoney. You're just a mougou like I said, and you won't be washing that out of my mouth. You've only got bad-good solutions for the regime in this country."

"Don't make me angry, Tara, eeeh! Don't get my back up, I say! You'll only make me worse!"

The other men got up to calm Comrade Démoney, who was now really riled up by Tara. "Let it go, Comrade Démoney. Let it go," they told him.

"Brothers, dear comrades," continued Tara, paying no heed whatsoever to Démoney's threats. "You know as well as I do— victory is not verbal. Words are to a woman's weakness what acts are to a man's courage. But Comrade Démoney here is just a loudmouth, yack, yack, yack! Yes, all he does is talk. He never makes any suggestions. Do you get what I'm saying? Not a single one! But the rest of us, we want action, not just someone yack-yack-yacking away! Personally, I think we need to take up arms."

"You're going too far, Tara!" the men shouted, disagreeing. Only Comrade Kissoko, a paunchy little guy with a glum expression and reedy voice, seemed to take Tara's side.

"I wholeheartedly agree with Comrade Tara," shouted Kissoko. "Either you're a winner, or you're a mougou. Victory and real change require action, not just palavering around or reading old newspaper articles. The only way to bring the regime down today is to take up arms."

"But you," added Tara, turning to Démoney, "you're no longer prepared to join the maquis. You're just a mougou!"

"Don't insult me, Tara. If you're looking for a fight, you'll get one."

"I didn't insult you," Tara corrected him.

The muddy veranda was on the verge of becoming a boxing ring. Thankfully, the comrades calmed Uncle down. Solemnly, he began, "I'm stunned, sickened even, that you'd call me a woman. That's a personal attack, isn't it? Is that the way to talk to your own comrades? You know very well how determined I am to bring down the regime. Are you ignoring the fact that it's no longer people like us who change regimes? The people no longer exist. There is only the international community. Do you understand, comrades—the In-ter-na-tion-al Com-mu-ni-ty!"

"Which means?" asked Kissoko, stroking his belly.

"Which means the richest people in the world. When they want to bring a regime down, they do it, and they don't even get their hands dirty! And us, we're just small fry compared to them; we're far too small to take up arms to attack anyone."

The pro-Démoney comrades applauded my uncle. One of them, Comrade Mitoumba, poured him a glass of matango to congratulate him.

"You're taking it too far," replied Comrade Bitoro. "You're right; we don't need weapons. We already risked our lives in vain with light arms during the ghost towns. Remember? These days, I'm Gandhi; I'm all for nonviolence, marches, and peaceful demands."

Squeals of laughter filled the air. I laughed too. I laughed because my comrades were laughing. I laughed because I wanted to be like them. I laughed because I saw my uncle's yellow teeth and realized that his rattan ndongo ndongo didn't really help whiten them at all. I laughed even more when I saw Comrade Kissoko, the short paunchy guy, reposition his belly between his thin frog-leg thighs so he could call Comrade Bitoro a naive dreamer and mock him more easily.

"Whatever happens, violence or no violence, we shall, and we must, continue to fight for this country and for our children," concluded Comrade Démoney.

They all applauded, recognizing the cause that had united them for so long.

IT'S A WINTER morning. It's so cold that my mother, Mbila, wants to talk to stay warm. So she decides to tell me about a few things that happened to Uncle.

My mother loves to yack-yack-yack away, but this time she gets straight to the point; I like it when she's direct. She tells me my uncle's life took a turn for the worse when his number one enemy, President Biya, was elected to run the country. She says quick-quick that she doesn't know all the ins and outs of all that business because she's not really into politics. All she knows is that the presidential election was strongly contested by both the opposition and the population. She tells me how her brother and his comrades kept saying all day long that there had been fraud, the ballot boxes had been stuffed, the ballot papers had been counted in the dark during a planned power cut. Crowds had gone out into the streets. Men of all ages, young and old, had built roadblocks with tires and set them alight. Those flames had lit up streets where the lights had stopped working a long time ago. The men had told their wives and children to stay home. Afraid, all the shopkeepers had locked up their little shops. Military forces, the mbéré, had gone out into the streets and shot at people, like in war movies. People had died just like that, for nothing. People had called it the ghost towns.

My mother comes back to President Biya. She tells me he's so firmly planted in the minds of more than one generation that people—some respectfully, others scornfully—even call him Papa. "They call him Papa, Papa Biya, Papa Paul," she says. But Uncle and his comrades, well, they don't call the president Papa. They prefer Elysée Barbie. Yes, I know this because that's what my comrades often called him when I was there. They said Papa Paul was a "Barbie doll controlled directly by the Elysée Palace in Paris."

The way they compared the president to those blond dolls really made me laugh, because I adored those dolls. I loved changing their outfits—claret-red evening dresses one day, multicolored swimsuits the next. And I simply loved brushing their long hair and feeding them with empty baby bottles.

My mother was being very kind to me one day and asked me what I wanted for Christmas. Without hesitating, I said, "I want a Barbie doll with long blond hair." She was horrified. Naturally, she outright refused to grant this wish. Instead of a doll with long blond hair, she got me an action figure from a Japanese cartoon that everyone was raving about, Goku from *Dragon Ball Z*.

❧

Barely two years after his appointment as a tax inspector, Uncle was pushed into early retirement. "What a load of nonsense!" he said, outraged. "Retirement at only thirty-five!" As far as he was concerned, it was yet another sign of intimidation.

To be honest, if you only consider early retirement from afar, it's not that bad—the National Social Insurance Fund, the NSIF, gives you a little mbongo every month, after all. But Comrade Démoney knew that queues at the NSIF are endless and that you need a truckload of patience in your belly to wait for your mbongo. That wasn't the problem, though; Uncle could easily wait. The real problem's when you see what you actually get for your early retirement—what they give you each month is as tiny-tiny as a crumb of bread.

That's why my uncle said his pension was as skinny-skinny as an AIDS patient. He talked like that because over there, AIDS was causing great misery: young people, old people, children, adults, everyone fell into its trap. But it was the younger ones who fell in deep-deep. Mbila said it was because they did naughty things. The joke went around that AIDS actually meant Ailment Invented (by white people) to Discourage Sex. Back in Switzerland, I said that in biology class one day. The teacher had asked, "Can anyone tell me what AIDS is?"

I raised my hand.

"Yes, Dipita, tell us."

I rolled my eyes like a chameleon from the marshland and chewed on the blue cap of my ballpoint pen. Then, with great determination, I summoned up all my courage and said, "AIDS is the Ailment Invented (by white people) to Discourage Sex."

The entire class burst out laughing. All my little schoolmates slid under their desks in fits of giggles. I was mortified. Perhaps I should have pulled some drawers over my mouth. It would have been easier. But it was too late.

"Quiet, please! Calm down!" the young teacher shouted, failing to bring the other children back under control.

Miss Rosalie Rey was usually very calm. She had red hair, pale skin, and a kind expression. However, like all teachers, she was mean to anyone who didn't pay attention. I didn't want to get into trouble with Miss Rosalie Rey; I wanted to apologize for answering incorrectly.

To my great surprise, instead of turning the page on the whole episode and swearing, scout's honor, that she would never let me speak again, Miss Rosalie Rey came over to me and quietly asked, "Dipita, where did you hear that?"

"Miss," I replied, looking down, focusing on my blue pen, still chewing the lid, "the last time I went to Cameroon, people were talking about AIDS a lot. Over there, they say it kills lots of people—everyone, even small-small children. My mother says it kills people because they do naughty things. You know what I mean, right, Miss? Naughty things. There isn't any medicine to cure that disease. So if it catches someone, too bad for them; it'll finish them off. Over there, Uncle Démoney is on early retirement. He says his pension is now skinny-skinny like an AIDS patient . . ."

My little classmates held their sides again, splitting themselves with laughter. The teacher turned red and smiled discreetly behind her hand. She was looking at me strange-strange, partly with pity, partly with pride.

"OK, Dipita. OK," she replied. "You seem to know enough about AIDS. Impressive. But you still need to learn a bit more. OK?"

"OK, Miss."

Uncle had added "pension as skinny-skinny as an AIDS patient" to his list of collateral enemies. But he hadn't seen it all yet—the worst was still to come. Even what little mbongo he got for his early retirement pension disappeared. The Elysée Barbie, under pressure from the French president whose name I never learned, had decided to privatize everything: water, electricity, air, forests, education, health care, chickens, goats, and even poor pensioners' mbongo. That's why Uncle no longer received his pension each month.

Knowing my uncle, I'm sure he'd have given Papa Paul a good thrashing with that ndongo ndongo toothbrush of his, given half a chance.

❧

What Mbila likes most about her older brother is his visionary side. "He's able to take a long-eyed look at tough situations," she says.

Back when he was a tax inspector, my uncle made some good contacts. "It's through someone that someone becomes someone," he'd say. Uncle knew lots of someones who could have made him a someone. Great salesmen who soon-soon conquered Europe, America, and the East. We call them feymen, swindlers. Politicians—assistant divisional officers, divisional officers, mayors, members of Parliament, ministers, and so on. Uncle even knew people who managed to hold all those posts at the same time. He said this accumulation of official posts was called taking too many seats at the table. "My dear Dipita," he added, "if you get into politics when you grow up—something I wouldn't be against—never take too many seats at the table. Remember, you'll only get too fat if you eat too much!"

My uncle looked sad whenever he talked about those sorts of things. And it made me feel bad too. There was a truckload of hate in my belly for people who took too many seats at the table. Seeing him sad, I wanted to cheer him up a bit, so I said, "Uncle, I'll never take too many seats at the table!" This promise made him smile, finally. He looked at me full of affection, and it made me feel good.

❧

Uncle had used his network of someones to help his sister escape to Europe, so she could become someone there too. Mbila tells me so herself—I don't even have to ask. She says it had all been organized by guys who claimed they were tackling poverty and exclusion among girls. Uncle called them the Philanthropists. He even called them the Benevolent Philanthropists because, as far as he was concerned, they were the Messiah in flesh and blood. These guys said they worked with the white people, the French. You see, when you say you're working with white people, no one even thinks you might be a feyman. So that's how people fall quick-quick into your trap.

Mbila explains that Démoney had told her, "Those people are good people. You can trust them. They've already saved several families from misery here by sending their children to Europe." He paused briefly to rinse his mouth out with some matango before continuing, "You know the Atangana family in Yaoundé. You know their wretched father who would come to our house in Douala every year to ask for some money and a few bunches of plantain. That family whose children didn't even know the way to school just a few short years ago. Well, they now have a big house in the middle of their village, in Ekélé. People call their house the Tower! Imagine that! That two-story house is a point of reference in a village where all the other roofs are made of straw. Ekélé doesn't have any electricity, so they arranged to bring it to their tower all the way from the city. And that's not all! The father, dear sister, well, he goes to Paris the way you and I go to the toilet! So tell me—do you think they achieved that level of prosperity with magic? No, o! The key to their success is their daughter, Amougou Atangana. It was the Benevolent Philanthropists who raised her up by sending her to France."

Now don't go thinking that Uncle was trying to persuade Mbila. She didn't really have a choice.

My mother always calls herself a dunce. Her time at primary school had been a total failure, and Uncle regretted having poured his money into it for nothing.

At the age of thirteen, like most teenagers, Mbila saw her chest take shape and start to raise-raise her T-shirts. Her "red wine" pushed her into all that women's business. But as those physical changes were taking place, Mbila was still stuck in second grade at primary school. How humiliating!

The children in her class at Saint Jean Bosco Primary School in Akwa teased her and called her Mama Mbila. All this made

19

my mother want to say bye-bye to school. She tried to explain this to Uncle.

"Papa, school's not really for me, o. I don't understand anything they say there. It's too complicated. Those white-people conjugations have lots of tenses. We don't have many in Bassa, but we speak just fine, eh?"

She fell silent, waiting for Uncle to reply. An inquisitive fly buzzed around and settled on her nose. Mbila brushed it off with the back of her hand, sending it packing.

She didn't dare look her brother in the eye. Out of respect, she never looked him in the eye. She cowered a few steps away. She stood neither too close nor too far away, ready to flee should he decide to hit her with his ndongo ndongo.

Uncle finally spoke. "And how do the other children manage?"

"I don't know, Papa," she replied immediately. "They must be geniuses."

"What do you mean?"

"I have to give up, Papa. And Mama Bilolo says I'm already a woman."

"So?"

"Well, that means . . ." continued Mbila, afraid. "That means I can already get mar . . . married. I can get married and have children and live with my husband. In peace. I don't want the other children to keep calling me Mama Mbila like I'm their mother."

At first, Uncle Démoney didn't know what to say about his sister's worries. He was surprised to discover that Mbila had decided to say bye-bye to her own education when so many children elsewhere in the neighborhood were desperately looking for ways to pay for primary school at the very least. Then my uncle smiled, reassured by his sister's decision. He didn't want long-long tongues one day accusing him of having stopped paying for his own daughter's education—him, a man who always got angry at parents who kept their girls at home. Uncle was actually pleased with his sister's decision; he wanted to send her off with the Benevolent Philanthropists. After all, when she suggested she get married, Mbila couldn't have expected him to agree. She didn't think the great Comrade Démoney would allow his sister's future to turn out like that, did she? Running a household, popping out kids one after the other, taking care of a husband at least twenty years her senior? Oh no, that wasn't going to happen. She had to leave. It was the golden opportunity to change her entire destiny, and the destiny of her family.

IV

I KNOW EVERY little detail of the rough white walls that make my cell a sealed cage. The door is as deep as the Lake Geneva embankments down by the Wilson Quay. I used to love running around there as a kid with my friend Saarinen, a chatty little Latino who reminded me of my uncle's son, my cousin Pitou.

Pitou was five years older than me but looked much younger. We liked to compare our heights from time to time by standing up straight, back-to-back. We noticed I was a bit taller. He must have had some sort of growth deficiency—well, that's what my mother thought. It was because Pitou didn't have enough calcium in his bones, she would say: "He needs to drink milk." I think she was right, because all he really ate were Auntie Bilolo's accra banana fritters.

During my long school holidays in Cameroon, the temperature would fall—at least in comparison to the rest of the year. It would only drop to around twenty-three or even twenty degrees Celsius, but my cousin couldn't stand it. "This weather is for white people," he would say, shivering. I took the opportunity to give him some thick sweaters from Europe. He pulled them on quick-quick like a tramp, but my woolen sweaters didn't seem to be enough to keep him warm, so he started to yack-yack. He talked about women who did naughty things with boa constrictors to get mbongo; strange men who went with sirens—the Mami Wata from the Wouri river—for a dime; men who raped madwomen in the trash to get a promotion; fathers who sold their children to a mysterious cult. My cousin had an endless repertoire of stories about witchcraft.

At first, those stories scared me. I couldn't sleep at night. I was haunted by images from Pitou's disturbing tales as I lay under my mosquito net. Auntie began to worry about me because I wasn't sleeping. I told her it was because of my cousin's scary stories. She smiled, hugged me, and begged me to stop listening to all that stuff. "My nkana," she said, "my little white boy, don't let yourself get carried away by that idiot Pitou's ideas." After that, whenever my cousin told me stories, I'd let them go in one ear and out the other. None of them stuck. Remembering all those things now makes me want to see my cousin again and ask him to tell me another story.

When Pitou realized that I no longer believed his lies about witchcraft, he started to tell me stories about so-called deviant behaviors. That's what he called them, deviant behaviors. He told me about the latest Bikutsi hits that made the hips of all the young women in neighborhood sway. He told me about a Makossa video where the dancers were almost naked and even showed their *thing* down there to the camera. He told me about children who hit their progenitors—at which point he always took great care to explain what he meant: "Their progenitor, you know." And when I'd protest, saying, "A parent is a parent; who cares about the progenitor," he'd reply, "Oh no, white boy Dipita. There's a reason the French language has two different words, parent and progenitor." Since I didn't want to get into the details about the difference between a parent and progenitor, or the importance of a progenitor compared to a parent, I'd leave it there and just let him go on, yack-yack!

"Holy cow, Cousin! Don't you get it? That kid beat up his own mother. Whack! Whack! Thwack! Like in the Chinese movies with Jackie Chan."

"Really?" I asked, skeptical.

"Yes, Cousin! He kicked her! Yaaaah! Yaaaah! He hit his own mama, the one who gave birth to him hard-hard like that in La-quintini Hospital in Akwa! Can you believe it! Unbelievable! Shit! You know what, Cousin?"

"No, spill," I said

"That guy's evil! It's obvious that kid's evil. Raise your hand to your mother? It's pure, simple evil. No, it's deviant behavior!" Pitou shouted.

"What?"

"*Deviant behavior*! Straight to hell! And I swear, even down there in hell, they won't want him," my cousin explained.

Since I didn't say a word and he really wanted me to gossip a bit more, he asked, "So, Cousin, are there kids like that over there in Switzerland, kids with *deviant behavior*, where you live?"

I honestly didn't have an answer. And even if I'd had one, I wouldn't have tried to pull the drawers off my mouth. I knew my cousin; silence was the only way to escape his interminable lectures. I just shrugged, disinterested, and he exclaimed, "Thank the Lord! It's good you don't have any *deviant behaviors* like that over there!" The way he emphasized the words *deviant behaviors* made me laugh.

I remember Auntie Bilolo too—her skin whitened with all those lotions and carrot-lemon-avocado oils made in shady labs in Lagos. In addition to burning her epidermis, Auntie burned her fingers frying accra banana in her smoke-blackened kitchen.

Sometimes I'd help her peel dozens of cooking bananas for the batter. They were called cooking bananas because they were the same green ones the monkeys in tropical regions like. I'd peel at least thirty and slip them into Auntie's wooden mortar. It was Pitou's job to mash them. *Dob! Dab! Dob!* He would bash the pestle furiously in the mortar. Short, sharp jabs. Cousin may have had a calcium deficiency, but he was strong, definitely much stronger than me.

Auntie Bilolo would collect the mashed bananas in an aluminum bowl. She'd sneak it away to her outdoor kitchen, a kind of cage made from rusty old sheets of corrugated iron nailed to wooden posts. The walls had been completely blackened by wood smoke. She called her kitchen her lab. That's where she'd hide away to prepare the batter for the accra banana, to make sure she was the only person who knew the recipe, her secret recipe. Considering the results, I think she must have added flour to the mashed banana—maybe some yeast too, but I'm not so sure about that. She didn't need to add sugar, though; the cooking bananas were already sweet enough.

After frying the accra banana, Auntie would flog them at the makeshift Ngodi-Akwa street market. She'd pile the accra banana into a tall pyramid on a pale-yellow aluminum platter flecked with spots of rust. She'd cover them with the old newspapers Uncle and his comrades left lying around on the muddy veranda. Huge oil stains would appear through the newsprint. I don't know why, but Auntie always said the grease marks were proof that her wares were top quality.

She would carry the pyramid of accra banana carefully-carefully on her head, balanced on a spiraled cloth. And that's when the most exhilarating part of her work would begin—she could balance her full platter without even needing to steady it. It seemed like magic to me, something extraordinary, like saying abracadabra. I was even more impressed when I saw her run or readjust her wrapper over her sagging chest.

I couldn't take my eyes off Auntie's platter of accra banana. You never know, I thought. I was always ready to catch it in case it fell.

Thankfully that never happened, and I eventually left Auntie's accra banana in peace. After all, balancing that platter was a key part of her work as a street hawker.

The muddy, slippery side alleys around the Ngodi-Akwa street market were filled with dozens of little vendors. "Hot-hot accra banana! Accra banana—hot-hot for everyonnnnnnnnne!" Auntie would shout at the passersby. Sometimes her voice would disappear among the shriller cries of the other hawkers selling all sorts of things: "Sweeeeets-cigarettes-chewin-guuuuuum! Sweeeeets-cigarettes-chewin-guuuuuum! Fried ground-nuuuuuuts! Fried groundnuuuuuuts! Hot-hot fried plantain! Waaaaaater! Mineraaaaaaal water! Alaska popsicles! Alaska popsicles! Ten-franc popsicles! Tight-tight bras for Mama's big lolooooooo! Cooooooooondoms! Condoms stoooooooop AIDS!"

When Auntie's voice was no longer loud enough to attract customers, I would take over, like the Olympic relay team on TV. With my little voice, I would shout as loud as I could. "Acraaaaaa bananaaaaa! Auntie Bilolooooooo's hot-hot acraaaaaa banan-aaaaa! Acraaaaaa bananaaaaa!" Auntie would cry with laughter. The street was noisier than a tramline construction site in downtown Geneva. It was loud, yes, but so much fun I didn't want to go home, not to the Ngodi-Akwa marshland or to the Pâquis neighborhood in Geneva.

Auntie would weave-weave her way through the precarious stalls selling fresh and smoked fish, all of it stinking. She would avoid the plastic mats on which women sold tomatoes and all sorts of vegetables: cassava, cocoyam, yams, sweet potatoes, ripe and unripe plantain, and much more. Holding my hand, Auntie would say, "Oh, Dipita, my nkana, watch out."

"Yes, Auntie! Yes, Auntie! I'm not going to walk on what people are selling."

Sometimes I would get scared when I saw termites, caterpillars, or grasshoppers still alive and kicking as they swarmed in 1.5-liter plastic Coca-Cola bottles.

"Hey, Auntie! Hey, Auntie! Do people eat those things here?"

"Oh yes, Dipita, people eat them. Meat is far too expensive at the butcher's here. Fresh fish is off-limits; it's so expensive. And even the price of bifakas, dry fish, is rising-rising. All we get is that dirty Wan-Chu frozen chicken, sent in big-big loads from China to kill us off. But your uncle and me, we don't like it. If we can't afford bifakas, we get some insects."

"And they're nice, Auntie?"

"They're nice-o! I'll cook them for you soon. Don't forget to remind me, OK?"

"Mm-hmm, Auntie."

In addition to the Ngodi-Akwa market, Auntie also sold her wares at the small building sites nearby, where the hardworking, muscly laborers sweat under the hot-hot sun. They put all their energy into making hollow cement blocks. They moved sand and bags of cement in metal wheelbarrows. They tipped out the sand, made wells in the heaps with their round-ended spades, and then poured in cement. They mixed it carefully and added water. Lots of water. Then they poured the mixture into cement block molds. The bigger ones were called twenties, and the smaller ones tens.

Auntie had a very good relationship with her cement block–maker customers, or her assos, as she called them. They called her Ma or Mother. It was their way of showing respect. But whenever one of Auntie's assos wanted to take advantage of her kindness by asking, "Oh, Mother, can you give me some credit? I'll pay you back tomorrow," she would always solemnly reply, "There's no credit today; come back tomorrow!" The rest of the cement block makers would split their sides laughing, gripping their spades.

I would watch Auntie flog her wares with ease and look forward to telling Mama what we'd done that day. Mama said the heat was deadly, so she always stayed shut up in an air-conditioned room in a hotel with several stars downtown. You'd think she was born there. Honestly!

Auntie didn't have any savings, but she did occasionally produce some mbongo from her pocket to top up Uncle's pension. Everything else went into a njangi the Ngodi-Akwa women used to protect the capital in their small businesses. And it worked! The proof was that Auntie Bilolo had sold her accra banana for years and her business had never failed. Even when all Comrade Démoney talked about was the devaluation of the CFA franc, structural adjustment plans, budget deficits, HIPCs, the IMF, the World Bank, and so on, Auntie continued to sell her wares.

One day, Uncle Démoney wanted to give me a few coins to buy myself some good-good accra banana from Auntie Bilolo, whose favorite phrase was "there's no credit today; come back tomorrow." He sneaked me into his room and told me to sit on the corner of his bed. I sat down, waiting. Without making a sound, Uncle slowly closed the door behind him. He turned the lock twice—*click-clack*—like we were being chased by local thieves. He padded silently toward me, as though trying not to stamp up any dust from the bare floor. Without saying a word, he sat down a hair's breadth away from me. He patted my head, then stood up again slowly, struggling with his aches and pains and rheumatism. He smiled at me and whispered, "My little Dipita, I want to show you something." Slowly-slowly he lifted one side of his old mattress. It was full of holes where sponges had been cut away for washing dishes. I immediately spied something: a small, dented, rusty tin. There was a slit in the top to slide mbongo in.

"Look," said my uncle solemnly, "this is my bank."

"Your bank, Uncle?" I asked a little too loudly.

"Ssssh!" he replied, bringing a finger to his lips, glancing left and right as though making sure no one had heard us. "Ssssh, Dipita! Walls have ears. We have to whisper. Quiet-quiet, OK?"

"OK, Uncle," I murmured almost silently, barely whispering, like I was playing that game where you swap secrets you can barely hear but split your sides laughing anyway. "But, Uncle," I continued, "banks aren't like that in Switzerland, you know. There are lots and lots of banks in Geneva: UBS, Crédit Suisse, and even the Migros supermarket bank! It's huge! It's beautiful! And the men and women who work there are rich-o! And they always wear suits and shirts and ties and drive cars. My mama said I have to become a banker when I grow up. That way I'll wear suits and shirts and ties and drive cars too."

"And she's right," agreed Uncle Démoney. "Yes, your mother is right. We'll need at least one doctor, one banker, and one pastor in the family."

"OK, Uncle. So if I've got it right, I'll be a banker in Geneva, and Pitou will be a doctor at Laquintini Hospital. That way he'll avoid deviant behavior. But there won't be a pastor in the family."

"Don't worry. With or without a pastor, God will have heard us. The main thing is that he makes our banker and doctor rich. Never forget, son—don't be like your mother; you have to remember to help your family when you grow up over there in Geneva. Because look here, there's nothing left in my bank."

Uncle stared at the little slit in his tin bank. It was heartbreaking. I felt sorry for him. That's when I realized he was entrusting me with a great mission. He wanted me to save the family because times were tough. If I don't do something, everything will go wrong, I thought. And then Uncle will get really angry with me. He might even stop calling me comrade.

I'd just seen my uncle's bank. It was no small matter—it was a secret. But I wasn't afraid to hide a secret deep-deep in my belly.

It would never come out because I wasn't a loudmouth yack-yacking like Pitou. Not even the political and administrative authorities' big bulldozers would be able to extract that information from my belly.

Would my uncle, who had trusted me enough to show me his secret bank, do the same now that I'm in prison? Has my mother had the courage to confess to him all the terrible things I've been charged with?

V

"MY DAUGHTER, don't they say, 'The Lord helps those who help themselves'?"

"Yes, Papa," Mbila had replied without looking Uncle Démoney in the eye.

"If they say, 'The Lord helps those who help themselves,' then I'm going to help myself, and I'm sure the Lord will help me in return. Won't he?" continued Démoney.

"Yes, Papa."

"To do that, dear daughter, I'm going to put all my savings into that Benevolent Philanthropist business, and you'll see—God willing, you'll go to the white people. Once you're there, you'll raise us up, won't you?" he explained.

"Yes, Papa," agreed Mbila.

As Mbila tells me all this, I laugh myself silly. She imitates Uncle's deep voice and village-chief airs. She widens her eyes and is his spitting image. I cry with laughter because, in my mind's eye, I can see him saying all those things to Mama.

There's still some tea in the pot on the little table in our lounge. Mama acts like a Bantu princess as she lifts it, even though she says it's to help her practice integrating in Switzerland. She adds two teaspoons of local honey to her cup and blows on the hot-hot tea before slowly bringing it to her rouged lips. They leave a mark on the rim of the flower-patterned cup.

"Where were we with that story I was telling you?"

"Eh, you were sixteen when Uncle tried to send you to France."

"That's right! Mm-hmm!" she murmurs, savoring her honey-sweetened black tea.

Mama continues. She tells me it all began one morning during the dry season. The sun was blazing down with all its might, and it was just over forty degrees in the shade. Uncle had handed her over like a package to two men. That was after talking to them for a long time next to the Immigration Police Station in Bonanjo, Douala.

It was an old building; the white paint had yellowed and was flaking off everywhere. Large patches peeled away, giving the walls a dilapidated air. At the front, there were a few benches where a crowd sat, obediently waiting to be seen. Mbila could easily see that some of them had been waiting for a long time. She even heard a toothless old mama nearby complain that she still hadn't been seen by the Immigration Police Station officials even though she had arrived early-early that morning, long before sunrise. That grandmama told Mbila that if you wanted to be seen before the others, you had to give your share of mbongo. But she didn't have any. That was why she was still there.

What those officials forgot, says my mother, was that after all she'd gone through, an old woman like that always has a truck-load of patience in her belly. No matter what you do, she'll wait quietly, stretched out on her long, bare wooden bench.

Mbila left the old woman in peace. She looked over at Uncle and his Benevolent Philanthropists. She saw him take a beige envelope from his pocket. He gave it to the two men. They checked it as discreetly as they could, like real feymen. Then, in exchange, they handed Uncle Démoney a small dark-green book. He flicked through it, licking his right index finger from time to time.

"It all happened quick-quick; a transaction was done, like on rue de Berne," explains Mama.

After his conversation with the Benevolent Philanthropists, Uncle seemed exhausted, like a boxer after a tough-tough round with Mike Tyson. He pulled up his trousers and tightened his belt, as though the transaction he had just completed had cost him a few kilos. Then, with the confident stride of a winner, he walked toward Mama, the two guys right behind him. He held out the dark-green booklet. "Here you go, Mbila," he said. "Here's your passport."

"And what was it like? Did you get to look at it?" I ask my mother.

"Yes, I opened it right away to see what it was like; I couldn't wait to see my photo."

Mbila had smiled when she had seen her passport. It looked authentic, and the information it contained was correct. The photo was indeed hers, the same as the one in her school file at Saint Jean Bosco, where her classmates had nicknamed her Mama Mbila.

Everything was correct—apart from her date of birth. It had been changed. Instead of August 4, 1976, it said August 4, 1971. Five years older! My mother had suddenly gone from sixteen to twenty-one! Mbila was surprised to discover that Uncle had changed her date of birth.

"But, Papa," she said to her brother, "I wasn't born on August 4, 1971; I was born on August 4, 1976."

"Don't worry about that," Démoney replied, looking away as though trying to avoid Mbila's questions.

"But, Papa," Mbila insisted, worried.

"I said don't worry about that! From now on, you were born on August 4, 1971, OK?"

"Yes, Papa," she replied, still looking at the ground.

"You were born on August fourth, nineteen seventy . . ."

"Nineteen seventy-one, Papa."

"There you go!"

Mbila takes a break from telling her story.

Stories like that, you tell them slowly-slowly, or there's the chance you'll lose your way and take innocent bystanders with you. That's why my mother wants to wait awhile, to make sure everything she has just told me sinks in properly. But I think she also needs time to find the right words.

She drinks her black tea. It mustn't be as hot-hot anymore. She takes a longer sip, then belches loudly. I hate that sound, so I grimace to make sure she knows it. But she couldn't care less. She tells me I'm not well integrated, because well-integrated people like her can belch loud-loud.

Mama sinks into her rocking chair. She lights a cigarette and inhales deeply, like it'll provide the oxygen she needs to breathe. I have to admit, I'm happy Mama is younger than her passport says. But it feels weird to suddenly have to take five years off her age. I realize I need to do the mental arithmetic to get her real-real age: 2002 minus 1971 equals thirty-one. But if you subtract Uncle's funny business, how old does that make her? Another quick sum in my head: 2002 minus 1976 equals twenty-six. So Mbila is only twenty-six when she tells me about her past—that's her real-real age.

I look at my mother lovingly—the way I look at Barbie dolls.

"But why did Uncle Démoney make you older?" I ask her.

"It's complicated, son, you know," she says.

"But I can understand, Mama."

"OK. Well, in Cameroon, you become an adult when you turn twenty-one. And Papa Démoney said I couldn't come here if I was a minor," she explains.

"So why don't you get a new passport now, with your real-real age?"

"Because it's too complicated. It's risky!" she replies.

"Risky?" I ask, puzzled.

"Yes, son, it's risky, very risky, in fact."

"But why?" I wonder.

"Come on; that's enough of your whys. It would be risky to do it now. That's all you need to know. End of story!"

I snuggle deep-deep into my pouf like a lazy mussel. There's only sadness in Mama's expression. Great sadness. I'm really trying to understand how she feels deep down, trying to put myself in her shoes. I imagine what it would be like to have been made five years older. From my perspective, an extra five years doesn't sound that bad. But when I start to do the sums with my own age, I realize it's not really that straightforward at all. For example, I was born in 1994, and Mama is telling me all this in 2002. First sum: 2002 minus 1994 equals 8. So I'm eight years old. Well, nothing surprising there; I have a birthday every year. OK. Now, what if you add five years to my age? A bit more mental arithmetic: 8 plus 5 equals 13. I'd be thirteen, just like that, for fun.

The thought of being older makes me smile. A thirteen-year-old can do all sorts of things an eight-year-old can't. My cousin Loud-mouth Pitou, for example, is thirteen, and Uncle says he's already able to think naughty thoughts when he talks to girls. But Uncle isn't totally right—my cousin told me he started thinking naughty thoughts about girls a long time ago. Meanwhile, I'm only eight, and I still don't have any thoughts like that.

I spend a lot of time playing Barbie dolls with my cotas, Blond Silvia and Brunette Romaine. They say I'm the perfect father for our dolls because I know how to take very good care of them. But which one of them is the dolls' mother? Or better still, who's my wife? "I'm Dipita's wife!" shouts pony-tailed Romaine.

"No, you're not! *I'm* Dipita's wife!" Silvia corrects her, her long blond fringe hanging over her face. They fight, neither of them wanting to give in. And while they fight over who's my wife, I continue to quietly brush our Barbie dolls' long hair. To get them to calm down, I say, "No, girls, I don't have any naughty thoughts about either of you. I love you both. But if you aren't nice and keep fighting, then I'll have to leave with Saarinen, because Barbie children don't like fighting and shouting."

VI

FROM MY PEAR-SHAPED POUF, I contemplate my mother's beauty. I look at her solemn features, her big eyes, her full lips, her flat-flat nose, her round cheeks, her long face. A typical Bantu face, as she says with a certain sense of pride. I watch her swing slowly to and fro in her rocking chair. Her voluptuous bosom, unjustly restrained in a tight black corset, sways in harmony. Her chest has always seemed in proportion to her derriere to me. Women with generous proportions like my mother are often called stunners. But my mother isn't simply a stunner; she's a knockout! Maybe that's why she's so popular on rue de Berne.

My mother rocks herself in her chair, back and forth, enjoying her cigarette. She puffs out large swirls of smoke toward the ceiling in our small lounge. Sharp-eyed, she studies the swirls as they vanish-vanish around the old bronze chandelier she picked up at the local flea market. She watches them like they hold the details of the rest of the story I'm waiting to hear.

Mbila isn't in a hurry. They're like that, Bassa girls who think they're Bantu princesses. You can't drag anything out of them. I stare at her as she smokes. I look-look at her and focus on her hair for a minute. She's had extensions grafted onto her own curly hair, painfully braided. I know it's the only way she can have long hair. Her own dry, curly hair never grows more than a few inches—not even with the help of the endless hair products she buys from her cota Charlotte, a Nigerian woman who owns an African hair salon in the Pâquis. Charlotte promises miraculous hair growth, but Mama's hair will never grow, not even if you put fertilizer on it.

Personally, I don't really like the look of my mother's short-short curly hair. I prefer her with long, straight hair. It makes her look more beautiful, sexier. I think the extensions give her the Western allure she's always after, even if she still acts like a Bantu princess.

After a few long minutes, my mother finally starts to tell me about her journey again. I get comfortable on my pouf and prick up my ears; I don't want to miss a thing. She goes back to the reason why Uncle changed her age.

She tells me how she listened very carefully to her father-of-a-brother on that dry-season day outside the Douala Immigration Police Station. As usual, she obediently pulled some drawers over her mouth when Uncle spoke.

"These two men will help you get out of here," announced Démoney. "Do whatever they ask. Obey them the way you'd obey me. I know them well, and you can trust them. The Benevolent Philanthropists are good people. Yes, they're extremely trustworthy. They've proved it again today. Just look at everyone here, waiting desperately in the hot-hot sun. But you, you've barely arrived, and you've already been seen. Isn't that a privilege, eh? Well, that was thanks to the Benevolent Philanthropists! They not only got you a passport, they got you a visa too, just like that, in the blink of an eye. That's it; you're ready to go, right now. All you need is a plane ticket. The Philanthropists will take care of that in a few hours. I gave them everything they need. They'll sort it all out. Don't worry."

When her father had finished his tirade, Mbila looked around. She saw the crowd waiting outside the Immigration Police Station. She saw the toothless old woman again, stretched out on a wooden bench without a back, lamenting the fact she still hadn't been seen. And Mbila realized she had been extremely privileged indeed. A sense of trust crept into her heart. Her respect for the Benevolent Philanthropists was now unconditional.

Uncle Démoney looked up at the sky. The rays from his sun god shone right in his eyes, making them sting, but he was determined to contemplate his god. He stared for a very long time. He raised his hands up to the heavens, like he wanted to receive something from on high. Something invisible, something mystical. He poured this mysterious gift over his face, like he was washing it. Then he opened his mouth wide-wide, as though about to yawn. He suddenly began to murmur almost silently to his sun god. He spoke in Bassa. Annoyed, the Benevolent Philanthropists stepped back, pretending they wanted to leave the father and daughter alone to say their goodbyes. A few gawkers outside the Immigration Police Station stared at Uncle in surprise.

Mbila, on the other hand, was frowning. Shame was having a whale of a time deep down in her heart. She didn't understand what he was doing either. She thought it might have been some sort of blessing ceremony. But was that how those sorts of blessings are performed? Publicly? In the middle of the city? She wanted to shout out to everyone around her that she didn't know this strange man, this man who could not only speak to the sun but also receive invisible gifts. But she didn't. She stood there, frozen despite the blazing sun.

Uncle finished talking to the sun and suddenly cleared his throat with great gusto and spat into his cupped hands. He mix-mixed his spittle and brought his saliva-soaked hands to Mbila's face.

It sounds pretty disgusting, and I can't stop from grimacing like I've just swallowed a truckload of bitter kola. It's worse than when my mother belches. While I sit there looking disgusted, Mbila says, "Son, if I could've died of embarrassment, I think I'd have dropped dead on the spot!"

With her father's saliva all over her face, Mbila clenched her buttocks tight-tight, because if she didn't, she might shit out her shame. More and more gawkers ran over to watch the free show. They didn't want to miss a single second of this strange ceremony. Some of them masticated like they were chewing gum. They were outraged and condemned this public display of witchcraft. "You really see it all in this country!" exclaimed the women, clapping their hands in astonishment.

Mbila's head drooped down-down onto her chest. She wondered when it would all end. Thankfully, she didn't need to worry for long. Démoney finished his prayer and sat down beside his daughter. The nosey parkers, disappointed the show was over, gradually drifted away, chattering about what they had just seen. One little shrimp of a woman pulled her kids close: "Shut your eyes children, the devil's on the prowl!"

But my uncle wasn't the least bit surprised by their reactions. He didn't even look at them. He just turned to his daughter and said, "Mbila, my daughter, you are blessed. The sun and his blessings now shine on your face. You shall have good fortune and good fortune shall dwell within you. You shall find success and success shall never leave you. You are blessed, my daughter. Never forget your family, OK? Never forget me, your father. Never forget your roots. May God guide your steps and may the sun light your path. Europe isn't easy, I know, but you are blessed."

With this blessing, Uncle waved at the Benevolent Philanthropists who had distanced themselves slightly. He took the big backpack one of them was holding. He slipped it onto his daughter's shoulders. She didn't know what Uncle had packed. He had organized everything without saying a word to her. Now, faced with a fait accompli, she had to simply obey Uncle and follow the Benevolent Philanthropists' instructions.

The backpack contained a few clothes, some cotton underwear that smelled strongly of the Ngodi-Akwa market, some manyanga, a palm-kernel oil body lotion, a few sanitary napkins for those women's things, a new-new New Testament, wooden rosary beads, a Coca-Cola merchandise watch, a small plastic box with a few accra banana (made by Auntie Bilolo, of course), and a bottle of ginger juice. Uncle Démoney readjusted the backpack to his daughter's height. He looked at her like a potter admiring his work. He hugged her tight-tight and whispered, "Bon voyage. Be good, my dear." Then he handed her over to the Benevolent Philanthropists the way you'd hand a package to your asso. So Mbila left Uncle and followed the two guys.

It was hot and the passing cars stirred up clouds of dust. Mbila walked fast, sweating like a street hawker, doing her best to keep up with the two men. They must have been in a hurry. Luckily for Mbila, they stopped under the shade of a mango tree for a while to catch their breath. She sneaked a glance at her companions and noticed how their heads shone like new-new leather in the sun. She wondered how on earth they could weigh themselves down with a shirt, suit, and tie under that hot-hot sun. They must feel like vegetables in a pot on Auntie Bilolo's wood stove, she thought jeeringly.

Apart from that, the Benevolent Philanthropists looked like those corrupt, careerist public officials riddling the country's perverted administration. They looked like the officials who took too many seats at the table that Uncle was forever criticizing; they looked like those cynical public officials who started their working day at eleven in the morning and finished at three in the afternoon, taking a well-deserved two-hour break to guzzle down beer and some roast chicken and fish. The sort of public officials who didn't do much to earn their keep, who mainly lived off tchoko, backhanders, you know. The sort of public officials who easily grew fat while the state coffers were kept on a diet. Anyway, the Benevolent Philanthropists looked like everything Uncle had always hated. That's why Mbila wondered why her father was hanging around with them like they were his cotas.

One of the Benevolent Philanthropists said to Mbila, "Don't worry, daughter of Mr. Démoney. I know your father well. When he was a tax inspector, he helped me greatly with my business. Unlike the men I meet now, I can testify and even swear on the head of my ancestors that your father is good! He's really not the kind of guy to be involved in all that tchoko business. He's a generous, serious, respectful, hardworking, upstanding, and above all, loyal man. He's exactly the kind of man this country needs to get it back on its feet. He's not like those idlers we see everywhere, right up to the top ranks of the administration. A real state scandal! A time bomb that could blow up the whole country!"

Downcast, the Benevolent Philanthropist lamented a system for which he personally had a huge appetite. He took a cloth handkerchief from his jacket pocket and wiped away the beads of sweat dotting his smooth scalp.

"Philanthropist Béfika and I are infinitely grateful to Mr. Démoney for what he did for us. That's why we did everything we could to make sure you could leave the country in peace. And in peace you shall leave. We not only got you a passport, we also got you a visa to enter France as a dancer."

Mbila couldn't contain her joy: "What? France? A dancer?"

"Yes, France. You'll be a dancer in France," Philanthropist Béfika replied.

"I'm going to the white people? I'll be a star? Me? Mbila?"

"Don't get too excited," Philanthropist Béfika warned. "Make sure you listen to Philanthropist Sandjon's instructions."

"The rules are simple," said Sandjon. "All you have to do is respect the group you're travelling with. If anyone asks you any questions, say you don't know anything. You're just a dancer. That's all. And above all, don't forget: you were born in 1971, not 1976. OK?"

"Yes! No problem! You can count on me."

"My friend Sandjon has explained everything," added Benevolent Philanthropist Béfika. "You just have to respect the people you're travelling with. Behave like an adult. And above all, once you're there, don't forget about us. Remember!"

Mbila smiled naively, the way any illiterate young woman who called herself a dunce would. She was as happy as if the waters of the Wouri river had turned to joy and now flowed through her heart. She thanked heaven, and above all Démoney, who had done so much to arrange her departure. She thought about all the mbongo she would soon earn as an international dancer in France and promised herself she would never forget her father.

But the rivers of joy wouldn't flow-flow through her heart forever. It wasn't long before Mbila felt a shiver down her spine. She thought about her new date of birth and slumped. Her face crumpled like a piece of paper scrunched up and thrown into an office trashcan. She looked up at the sky. She wanted to see if the sun god was still there. You never knew, maybe he would grant her blessings her uncle had forgotten to request. But nada, the sky was empty. Hollow. She felt uneasy about it all.

She was even more unsettled by the fact she was supposed to go off to the white people that very night. She was leaving on the sly. No one had been told about her departure. She couldn't quite take it in. It was like an abduction, a kidnapping. An abduction planned by Uncle Démoney, the architect of her life.

Uncle had carefully kept the trip under wraps to make sure that evil spirits—the forever jealous; the dissatisfied disciples; the jobless wasting away, watching others progress while they mark time; the all-for-me-nothing-for-others—didn't sabotage his daughter's good fortune. He'd woven this good fortune together with his own hands, inch by inch, and used up the last of his savings, as well as those of his wife Bilolo.

Mama was of course happy to go to France, every young African's dream. But she would also have liked the chance to say one last goodbye to her friends in Ngodi-Akwa before getting on the plane. She would have liked to give her sister-in-law-of-a-mother, Auntie Bilolo, one last long hug. She would have liked to help her fry accra banana one last time and sell them at the local market. Auntie would have given her pearls of wisdom to wear at all times. Woman to woman, Auntie Bilolo would have gone over a lot of things Mbila already knew, of course—things she'd already drummed into her—but which were worth repeating nonetheless. Like an underground feminist, Auntie would have whispered, "My dear daughter, never trust a man! They're all the same you know! Awful!" And they would both have laughed their marshland feminist laugh.

The next morning, Mbila called her brother to tell him she had arrived in France. Uncle was overjoyed. He was pleased to hear his plan had been a success. He thanked the heavens. He immediately told Auntie Bilolo about Mbila's departure. Auntie shrieked with joy. She promised to tell the entire neighborhood quick-quick.

My mother is certain that word of her departure for France had been breaking news in Ngodi-Akwa that morning, running like red ticker tape across all the residents' brows all day long. She says she must have been the talk of the town that day. They no doubt talked on and on about it: hidden away in those ramshackle houses; in the piss-scented side alleys; in the bars for drunken bums; at the Senegalese and Nigerian street stalls; in the PMUC betting kiosks where hustlers dream of winning billions; in the muddy side alleys at the market where Auntie flogged her accra banana; on the building sites where the cement block makers wore themselves out for a rat's pay; and even as far away as the farmyards where the loudmouth roosters ruled the roost.

It must have been good news for some and bad for others. One thing was certain, however; they were all calling Uncle Démoney every name under the sun. They called him a sly little fox, a sneaky devil, you name it! They even said he was a witch doctor because they thought you had to be one to be able to hide that sort of news.

People could really let rip when they wanted to, o! They could stretch their mouths open like a piece of gum, but Uncle couldn't care less. It wasn't worth worrying about. The only bad news would have been if Mbila had been sent back, if she'd been stopped at the airport for forgery and use of forged documents. Uncle knew very well there was something dodgy about the Benevolent Philanthropists' network. He knew it wasn't entirely kosher.

The Benevolent Philanthropists had managed to sneak Mbila into an extremely popular traditional music group, M'veng and the Bikutsi Killers, as a dancer.

They were off to Paris, where their beloved fans in the diaspora were dying for their two-week tour. Every time the group travelled to the West, its numbers swelled disproportionately, like garri when you add a lot of water. The European tours were an excellent opportunity to send an extra dozen or two "dancers" and "musicians" with the regular group members. Over the years, M'veng had established itself as the most successful human smuggling operation on the illegal migration circuit in

Cameroon. And when you're the best smuggler, you look reliable to anyone wanting to escape hell. So you can ask for a lot of mbongo to seal the deal. In Mbila's case, they had received several thousand CFA francs via an intermediary—Démoney's Benevolent Philanthropists.

For M'veng and the Bikutsi Killers, the dancers were actually their main line of business. Those girls could spin their generous booties like weathervanes in the cold-cold wind. They were called the Bikutsi Killers or the Bi-ZiZi Killers because men always started thinking naughty thoughts as soon as the girls hit play on their booties. And those men became very generous with their cash, showering the girls with new-new banknotes. But to become one of those hot-hot dancers, you had to be twenty-one. So that's the real reason Démoney added a few years to Mbila's age.

VII

MY MOTHER GOES into the kitchen. I don't know what she's doing in there instead of telling me the rest of the story; I'm dying to hear what happened next. I watch her as she walks. Her curvy derriere sways with each step. I realize it's why she would have made the perfect Bi-ZiZi dancer—she doesn't even have to try to roll-roll it quick-quick. The movement comes naturally to her; her bootie simply sways without being asked.

When Mama comes back into the lounge, she picks up the tube of hand cream sitting on the little table beside her rocking chair. She squeezes a blob onto her palms and carefully massages it in all the way up to her wrists.

Mama loves pampering herself—a Bantu princess must always look her best. She makes sure she has everything she needs to look fabulous. She spends hours and hours in the bathroom before she goes out on rue de Berne—usually at night—to passionately practice her profession as a wolowoss. Seeing her spend all that time in the bathroom makes me realize that to do well in a job like hers, you need a lot of me time. That's why she's never far from her friend Charlotte, the hairdresser. Charlotte does her hair well-well, so well that people think it's Mama's own hair.

Our bathroom is chock-full of beauty products: a huge plastic jar of shea butter labeled "African beauty—to keep your skin naturally dark"; Nivea, L'Oréal, Yves Rocher, and other types of cream to add a Western glow to the beauty spot she wants to keep dark-dark; day creams and night creams and even a few afternoon creams; antiblemish ointments; makeup and nail polish removers; a thousand shades of nail polish—red, blue, green, pink, orange, rainbow; various soaps and lotions; not to mention all the waxing products she's forever using to tame her abundance of hair. The common denominator for all these products is the "keep out of reach of children" warning.

Yet it's all within my reach. When Mbila's not around, sometimes I take one of her lipsticks to add a bit of color to my thin lips. Or I paint my nails, apply a face mask, or use some of her shampoo, even though my head is shaved. I often try on her wigs. And you know what? I love seeing how much I look like her.

"Keep out of reach of children"? My mother has never considered me a child. Even now, it feels like I've always been her roommate, or better still, her business partner. She regularly calls on my services to wax her eyebrows, blow-dry her hair, or pick out a dress that'll get her as many clients as possible in one night. On top of the beauty treatments for Bantu princesses, I've helped with PR too. She's asked me to politely send a few people packing—clients who were a bit too pushy, or women trying to collect debts early-early in the morning. Mama hides behind our front door as I look her debt collectors in the eye and say with a straight face, "Mama isn't here. She went away for a few days." After that, they retreat at the sound of my humble yet firm voice.

It's nice to feel important, indispensable. Being my mama's business partner and PR manager makes me feel as confident as a two-story tower. I love being treated like an adult.

My mother can tell me about her past because I'm her partner, and she trusts me fully. I don't spill the beans like those ladies in hair salons. Mama knows I've always got a pair of drawers tight-tight over my mouth. As tight as a girdle! She knows she can trust me; she's seen how well I've done all the jobs she's given me. I don't even need to ask her to promote me and do it quick-quick. She's already promoted me to the position of . . . psychologist! That's how she's made me a *someone* too.

I'm taking this new role very seriously. I listen to Mama like a professional, nodding and saying "hmmmm" a lot. I even ask the odd question, just to make sure I get all the ins and outs of her story.

My patient Mbila lights another cigarette and continues.

A two-week tour in France as a dancer was not going to be enough for Mbila to put some money aside and restore the reputation of a family bogged down in poverty. It definitely wasn't going to be anywhere near enough to puff up the chest of someone like Uncle Démoney, who was determined to escape the hardship he blamed on the political and administrative authorities and even the president of the republic himself. So Mbila could either stay in France illegally and live in fear of immediate expulsion, marry a man with papers (preferably a white man), or return home to Ngodi-Akwa after just two weeks on tour with M'veng and the Bi-ZiZi Killers. The last scenario simply wasn't an option. Uncle Démoney would drop dead from a massive heart attack if he saw his sister return so soon. And if a massive heart attack didn't get him, he'd simply take his own life, because that sort of shame is unbearable. Even his sun god would understand and forgive him. So Mbila had to do whatever she could to stay in France.

But what could a girl like Mbila do to stay in France, a country she knew only by name? The Benevolent Philanthropists hadn't told her what to do if you wanted to stay with the white people. They had only repeated a few hackneyed phrases like "Respect the members of the M'veng group and do everything they ask you to." That had been their mantra and Mbila had followed it to a T. She even gave the lead singer, Oyono Bivondo, the one thing she'd carefully preserved until the age of sixteen: her virginity. Oyono took-took it like it had been waiting for him alone.

She doesn't have a single regret. "Oyono was too handsome to refuse," she says.

She'd found it easy to follow the Benevolent Philanthropists' instructions and offer her sweet red bean to a charmer like Oyono, who had swept her off her feet. Mbila had been proud to give her red bean to this excellent specimen of a Black male. That's why she wasn't shocked or even hurt when, a few days later, she realized she'd only been the latest in a long line of conquests for a man who was only too happy to gobble up every new-new bean sprout in the group.

In 1992, M'veng helped Mbila and twenty-three other men and women land on European soil. Some of them left the group as soon as they arrived at Charles de Gaulle Airport. They were lucky; their families or acquaintances were waiting for them. That's where their adventure with M'veng ended. Of course, that wasn't the case for Mbila, who had only the sun god to help her on her way. She was hoping for a miracle during those two weeks. Well, she could live in hope, couldn't she? Hadn't Uncle Démoney prayed to his sun god to light her path? Hadn't he anointed her with his holy spittle? Hadn't he prophesied her blessing and prosperity? And if Amougou Atangana had made it in France, why shouldn't Mbila? Mbila was expecting her share of miracles within two weeks. She hoped she might meet a nice gentleman who would want to marry her or hire her as a maid. She even hoped she'd get to walk those four-legged creatures she hated so much. She hoped she'd get a job washing dishes or at an undertaker's, even. Why not? After all, once you were in Europe, anything was possible.

～

One night after another wild M'veng and Bikutsi Killers concert in a dodgy neighborhood on the outskirts of Paris, Mbila spotted the eldest Atangana daughter in the crowd. Amougou Atangana was the Benevolent Philanthropists' crowning glory. She had done so well in Europe she'd built a two-story tower in the middle of her village, Ékélé. She had made Paris her father's second home. He went there whenever he pleased.

"Amougou! Amougou! Amougou, my sister!" Mbila shouted in her thick tropical lilt.

The young woman looked all around her, trying to figure out where the voice was coming from. Mbila could see that Amougou recognized her voice. Amougou looked left and right again and when she saw Mbila swinging her arms round and round like a windmill, the way people do back home, she leaped off her chair and ran to greet her.

"Oh, Mbila, my sister! Mbila, my sister!" she ululated. "What are you doing here? It's so nice to see you!"

"Atangana! Amougou Atangana, daughter of Pa Atangana who became Atangana of Ékélé Tower, Atangana the Parisian! Oh, my sister, you're so beautiful!"

Amougou Atangana was the very definition of Black beauty. The young woman teetered on sky-high stilettos. Her elaborate makeup created contours too narrow for her Bantu face. You might have said she was Fulani. An afro wig crowned her head, giving a 1970s disco vibe. Her big earrings helped elongate her neck, making her look a little like a Padaung woman. A skin-tight, short-short sunflower-yellow dress did its best to cover as much of her body as it could. The dazzling yellow contrasted starkly with Amougou Atangana's dark-dark—too-dark—skin. The skin-tight skirt revealed beautiful, long, slender, and above all, bare legs—not a hair in sight. When Mbila saw Amougou's smooth-smooth legs, she felt a slight shiver of dread at the thought of the fine hairs on her own legs. Mbila realized then that if you wanted to be beautiful for the white people, you had to get rid of all that hair. But back in Cameroon, she thought, men went weak at the knees at the sight of a hairy woman.

"I didn't want people to think I was an unintegrated villager; that's why I started to wax myself good-good," Mama tells me.

"Oh, you're so beautiful, Amougou! I'm so happy to see you here, in the flesh, my sister! It's been so long," said Mbila.

"Yes, little sis, it feels like forever! But tell me—is everyone back home well? Uncle Démoney? And Auntie Bilolo? And Ngodi-Akwa? And the country? And Papa Paul, our president? Is everything OK?" Amougou asked.

"Everything's fine. Everything's fine, my sister. No bad news. Démoney's fine, even if his early retirement has him cursing the entire country, from Papa Biya to the little mice in Ngodi. He curses everyone. His wife says he's going mad. Apart from that, he's fine. Maybe that's why he wanted me to leave, to make sure he didn't lose his mind entirely. You know what I mean, sister, right? Life back home is hard-hard now," Mbila explained.

"I know exactly what you mean, little sis. When did you arrive?"

"Three days ago," said Mbila.

"Just three days ago! Let me give you a big hug to take in the fresh-fresh smell from back home before you lose it in the beauty product aisles here." The two women hugged, overjoyed. They embraced each other the way they do in our villages.

"But, little sis, who helped you leave?" Amougou asked, clearly curious.

"Well, I came here as a dancer," Mbila replied, whispering like it was a state secret.

"With M'veng and the Bikutsi Killers?" asked Amougou, still as curious.

"Yes, that's them."

"Oh, I see. I see. So that means the Philanthropists helped you leave?" Amougou continued.

"Yes, yes. They did. Uncle Démoney doesn't just call them the Philanthropists; he calls them the Benevolent Philanthropists! You should hear him when he gets going—yack-yacking on about *his* Benevolent Philanthropists. He only ever sings their praises. He says they're good people. That you can trust them, blah, blah, blah. But he said that after the M'veng tour, I'll be able to find a white man, stay here, and become rich. You know what I mean, big sister, right?" said Mbila.

"Yeah, I get it!"

"You get? Get what?" the younger woman asked.

"Get it! I get it. It means I understand," Amougou explained.

"Oh, OK! I see. That's good. You know, big sister, I'm really counting on you to help me. You're the only person I know here."

Amougou Atangana's face suddenly fell like she had just swallowed a kilo of bitter kola. Even her makeup lost its shine. The joy that had lit up her face a few minutes earlier suddenly evaporated. She forced a smile, but Mbila realized that if Amougou looked-looked like that, then something wasn't right.

"Is something wrong, big sister?"

"No, nothing. I just want to make sure you know that if the Philanthropists brought you here as a Bikutsi Killer with M'veng, you'd better be prepared to repay them. You know what I mean? You'll have to give them their money back."

"What? Repay them? But repay them what? They say they help people escape poverty, but you have to give them money? That can't be right!"

"Yes, little sis, that's how it works. In this world, no one ever does anything for free. Charity only exists in the Bible."

Amougou scowled like she wanted to yell at God for having placed Mbila on her path. She dragged her little sis into a corner.

Oyono, the lead M'veng singer, was taking his time posing for photos with beautiful fans beside the stage where the concert had just ended. Mbila looked at him and remembered what they had done the night before. If she could have, she would have gladly offered him her bean again, but it wasn't really the time to be thinking about all that. At the other end of the stage, young people were still going wild to Bikutsi beats. The women shook their generous booties like an invitation to the male population, who didn't hesitate to come and rub against them. It was what my cousin would have called deviant behavior, but those were the rules of the game. That's the way we dance—that's our Bantu ballroom style.

Amougou was on edge. She really wasn't in the mood for watching the frenzy. She told her little sis to sit down on a white plastic chair opposite her.

"Listen carefully, little sis. I came here the same way. I arrived in France as a Bi-ZiZi Killer. The Philanthropists arranged everything. And right here, right in this room, several other girls arrived as Bi-ZiZi Killers with the group too. So if you came with that network, then you'll have to do what the others did. You'll have to work for at least two years. Depending on the number and, above all, the quality of your clients, you'll be able to repay the Philanthropists every franc they spent on you. You know what? I'm not sure Uncle Démoney could have given them enough money for your trip. I think he'll have had to accept a few clauses in the contract, like getting you out on credit and then making you pay off the debt. That's why you'll have to be prepared to work hard to pay it all back. That's what all the girls here do before they start earning their own money. And that's what I had to do to get where I am today too."

"That won't be a problem at all, big sister," Mbila replied, bringing her hands together respectfully. "I'm a hard worker. You know that back home we've all got hard work in our blood.

And, big sister, we don't come to Europe, to Mbeng, to sleep, do we? We come to Mbeng to get mbongo. So if I have to work, I'll work."

"OK. Good. So that means the Philanthropists prepared you well. It's good they did, because that's not the case for most of the girls who turn up here. Anyway, I'll just remind you, it's easy. Oyono, the lead singer with M'veng, will send you to Geneva in Switzerland to get you started. The work's easier there; the pay is good, and the clients aren't as difficult. If you do a good job in Geneva, you'll be able to pay off your debt in less than two years. Once you've repaid your debt, you can decide whether you want to come back to Paris or stay in Geneva. It's up to you, little sis. All the M'veng girls pass through Geneva! I worked there for three years before coming back to Paris. I'd advise you to start right now, before you even leave for Switzerland. Find your first client now, tonight if you can."

"Client?"

"Yes, yes. Find your first client now. The rates are easy to remember. Fifteen hundred francs for a full night, seven hundred francs for a good service down-down below, and four hundred francs for a simple suck. There you go; those are the rates. You're young and beautiful, so I'm sure you'll be fine. I reckon you'll get as many clients as you want. Oh, I forgot—if you want to stay out of trouble with the girls who've been around a bit longer, you'd better avoid two things. First, no playing around with the back door. Second, don't undercut the rates I've just given you. It's unfair competition! And believe me, little sis, if you follow all my advice, you'll be fine. That's it. Welcome to Europe, and good luck!"

With that, Amougou Atangana, daughter of Pa Atangana who became Atangana of Ékélé Tower, Atangana the Parisian, disappeared. Mbila never saw her again. Ever!

Mbila sat there stunned, like an apprentice street hawker. Speechless. Mute. She had lost her tongue. She squeezed her buttocks tight-tight on that plastic chair because a huge hullaba-loo had just begun in her belly. Her big sister Amougou's revela-tions bubbled around in her head like a fizzy tablet in a glass of water. She looked all around her, searching for someone to ask for help. She felt her armpits moisten with a cold sweat that reeked of fermented palm wine. The fine hairs on her legs stood on end; she was so angry.

The image of her big brother abandoning her in the hands of the Benevolent Philanthropists flashed before her eyes again. She relived the moment her brother had given her the passport with her new fake age. She relived the benediction her father had per-formed with his spittle in her honor in front of a thousand onlook-ers. She could see Démoney clearly in her mind's eye, and a truckload of anger roared into her belly. If she had spotted him anywhere in the vicinity, she'd have roasted him alive like a grass-hopper for dinner. Démoney! Oh, Pa Démoney! Did he know about the shady terms of the travel arrangements he had made with the Benevolent Philanthropists he praised so highly? And if he had been informed of all the consequences in advance, had he decided to play the "I-sell-my-daughter game" nonetheless? Had he agreed to turn her into a cheap-cheap orange for people to squeeze out just like that, right to the last drop? Had he changed her real-real age from sixteen to twenty-one so she could sell her bean up there in Mbeng, in France?

No, Mbila didn't want to believe Uncle could have done any of those things to her. Her eyes welled up, and tears ran down her cheeks. Dismay and distress were etched on her face. She searched for a word in her own language, in Bassa, a word that could de-scribe everything that was happening to her. Hou nson, the worst kind of shame. That was all she could find.

In this sort of situation, when you feel that hou nson, you have to stay calm-calm and try to find a solution. In Mbila's case, there were only two options. Two very simple options, in fact. Either she went back to Ngodi-Akwa, or she continued her adventure, accepting all the conditions it entailed. Go back to Ngodi-Akwa? She'd never do that. She didn't even need to mull it over during a long-long lunch from noon to two o'clock to see Uncle glare at her in her mind's eye or hear the mocking laughter of everyone she hadn't said goodbye to before fleeing to Mbeng.

All of a sudden, the only reasonable solution—reasonable because it was the only one—was to continue the adventure and become a wolowoss. That was it. The word had been let loose in her head and thundered around it like a village drum—pros-ti-tute! From that point on, it had to stop being a cuss word. It had to be freed of any negative connotations and become an integral part of her life, her flesh, her bones, her very being.

My mother says there are some things in life she cannot forgive, not even if you offer her a crate of waxing creams. She wants to talk about what Uncle did to her; I can see it in her eyes. I can see how much it still affects her, and I think it always will. That's why she's never given Uncle his share of forgiveness. She's never raised him up the way he wanted, not even with a little-little Western Union. Nothing.

But Démoney wasn't the only one involved in all that business. What about Oyono? Oh! That macabo Oyono! That bastard to whom she had given her most precious possession! No, it wasn't just the most precious thing; it was also the most delicious thing she had within her. Down there, that fleshy, moist golden-red bean planted between her slender thighs. Like a sex-mad bulimic, he had tasted it all with his hard-hard thing, muscles tensed and determined, hip thrusts as merciless as they were precise, profound, very profound indeed. With each rhythmic thrust, the same sound: *top! top! top!* Then, all of a sudden, he had let out a violent, raucous cry, like a Zulu warrior. He had poured out everything he had down there. So plentiful, thick, ardent, like cassava pulp, Mama recalls. Oh! That Oyono! Oyono the Charmer! Oyono the scoundrel, whom she couldn't refuse. If Auntie Bilolo ever found out, she'd be beyond disappointed and ask, "My daughter Mbila, did you forget that you should never trust a man?"

My mother says she doesn't regret the naughty things she did with Oyono at all. He really knew what he was doing. But what she is angry about is how that macabo Oyono turned her into a whore in Geneva. It still makes her absolutely furious. She says she pictured herself lying on a bed, legs spread wide, buck naked, feeling a draft penetrate her from time to time. She pictured herself lying on the same bed, staring at a ceiling that was probably white. She saw herself staring at it to take her mind off those men. Those men who'd file in, one after the other, and lie on her, slimy, savage perverts with their hard-hard things. She imagined herself staring at the ceiling to take her mind off their breath and, above all, to avoid seeing their faces, so she wouldn't remember them. That was what she had thought prostitution was like.

Still sitting on the plastic chair, Mbila had thought about Oyono again as he stood there posing for photos on the other side of the room, surrounded by admirers. Oh, that bastard! He had jumped her last night with the sole purpose of checking the quality of the goods he was going to put on the Geneva sex market. That bastard! That moron! That son of a bitch! That . . . Mbila spat out every insult her heart could find.

VIII

THIS AFTERNOON, I don't feel like going down to the big carpentry workshop where they try their best to prepare us for life back on the outside. Down there, you plane, carve, saw, glue—again and again. They say it prepares us for successful reentry into the labor force after a few years behind bars. Plane, carve, saw, glue, glue! A bit like trying to glue the scattered fragments of your life back together after tearing through it like a cornfield yourself. I really want to believe anything's possible after prison, even if, in reality, I feel like I'm the only one who does. A lot of guys here think they'll be back after a few months, or even days, of freedom. When I talk to them, I wonder if they haven't signed up for a life membership to prison. I'm determined that won't happen to me—there's still a lot I want to do. I have to help my uncle. And time in Champ-Dollon Prison isn't going to stop me.

I never really felt I was part of Uncle and Mama's big falling out. That's brother-sister stuff, or father-daughter stuff even. And don't they say in Ngodi-Akwa that you should never put yourself between a rock and a hard place? I won't be poking my nose in their business.

I understand that some of the things Uncle did to Mama were unforgivable, but I won't be throwing the first stone. I can't

59

exactly hold charges against him forever. My mother already sentenced him to zero financial support. His dreams of prosperity have already crumbled once. I don't want to add to that. No, I don't want to add insult to injury because, as a prisoner myself, I have a pretty good idea of what it'd be like to serve a sentence for a crime twice. And if it hadn't been for his dodgy network, Mbila wouldn't be living in Switzerland now, and I'd never have been born in such a rich country, far from all that misery. So why stone my comrade Démoney?

"Doing time in prison isn't the end of the world," repeats our supervisor, a tall guy with shoulders as wide as a wardrobe. He says it with such conviction you'd think he'd been in prison too—planing, carving, sawing, gluing, and regluing the pieces of his life. Mind you, his pep talks—almost predictable now—have encouraged me to spend more time in the workshop. This afternoon, however, despite desperately wanting to build a future after Champ-Dollon, I'm staying in my cell, glued to my bed, reflecting on my past, frozen, sunken-eyed, semiconscious, sentimental, distracted.

Mbila says she served a long sentence for a crime she never committed: all in all, two years of forced prostitution on rue de Berne, Geneva. She worked relentlessly to pay off a debt she never took on. She gave it everything she had, forced herself to be professional even when she was at her lowest. She never complained, never grumbled the way other teenagers her age would have. But how could she have complained? To whom? And what would she have said? Where would she have started? Who would she have reported first? Uncle Démoney, the father who only wanted a little extra on top of his tiny-tiny pension? The Benevolent Philanthropists, those unscrupulous feymen who got rich off the backs of the poor? Oyono, the charmer with an insatiable dick? The magnificent M'veng musicians with murky undertones? Her "big sister" Amougou Atangana, the daughter of Pa Atangana, Atangana of Ékélé Tower, Atangana the Parisian? Who would she have reported to the Geneva police? And what sort of risks would it have involved? Wouldn't the police have just put her on the first plane back? So many unanswered questions buzzed around her teenaged head, sneakily made a few years older. It would have been too dangerous to go to the police. That's why Mbila simply decided to pull some drawers over her mouth.

Yes, going to the police was far too risky. So Mbila got her dark-green passport back after two years as a sex slave. It had been carefully guarded by Oyono Bivondo, a key link in the despicable chain that trafficked women. He may well have been a dirty bastard, but he was a man of his word.

Oyono appeared before Mbila late one night. She was sitting at the bar in the trendy Bohème Club on rue de Berne. That's where the girls, squeezed into their tight corsets, arranged to meet their clients—guys left wanting by frigid wives, guys almost crippled in one arm from permanent masturbation. Mbila was sitting on a high stool, legs perfectly smooth and neatly crossed.

The dim, red lights were in perfect harmony with the jazz lounge music float-floating through the club. The gentle tones of the legendary Miles Davis's "Blue in Green" brushed the damson damask walls before fading into the room. Mbila allowed herself to be carried away by the soothing harmonies. It was the perfect remedy to clear her head of all those unanswered questions that tormented her.

"Well hello, my darling Mbila," Oyono said, standing right behind her. "There you are! At last! I've been looking for you everywhere. But your phone's off. Everything OK?"

Even if she'd been deaf, Mbila would have recognized her Casanova's voice anywhere. So she kept her little backside stuck-stuck to her stool.

"I've got some good news for you," Oyono said.

Mbila was all too familiar with Oyono's "good news." It was usually only good news for him. Any time he hooked a big client—like a rich businessman, rich and old, sometimes too old—he'd rush to share his "good news" with young Mbila. It was good news for Oyono because he'd make good money, and in one way it was good news for Mbila too because it would help write off a good chunk of her debt.

"So what's this good news, then? One of your good clients, I assume?" the young woman asked, disillusioned.

"Short reckonings make long friends," Oyono replied calmly.

"What's that supposed to mean? Just tell me."

"What I mean is you're free now, darling. Free. You have paid your debt, and now you're free."

Mbila wasn't that gullible. She knew you couldn't just take that kind of news at face value. It glittered far too brightly to be real-real gold from Katanga. After all, you had to expect a guy like Oyono to tell a few lies. Anyway, she didn't even know how much she owed. She just knew she had to work—hard-hard—for at least two years to pay off her debts.

A big smile lit up the little Bantu woman's face quick-quick when, all of a sudden, Oyono held out her passport. It all started to become much clearer. The words on the front of the passport— *République du Cameroun* and Republic of Cameroon—were proof it really was a Cameroonian passport. It started to feel real. No more yack, yack, yack! Oyono Bivondo offered her the little dark-green booklet Démoney had given her two years earlier outside the Immigration Police Station in Douala, Cameroon.

Mbila took the passport from Oyono, snatching it out of his hand. She was shaking all over. She was so overcome with emotion that she hesitated before opening it. She looked at Oyono first, afraid and suspicious. Nodding, Oyono granted her the permission she hadn't really been requesting. She took a deep breath in, breathed out again, and finally decided to open it.

She saw her country's national emblem on the first page, a sort of misshapen shield hiding two crossed fasces, drawn-drawn in opaque shades of red, green, and yellow, the national colors. Mbila felt a stabbing pain in her gut. Were the two Roman fasces in the national coat of arms ripping her open? The pain in her aching belly made her grimace. She also saw the weighing scales printed on her passport, a symbol for justice and equity in Cameroon. So that's what must have made Démoney laugh.

Mbila turned the first page and saw her information. It really was her passport. She recognized her face in the photo. She recognized that young girl's face, the one the other children at Saint Jean Bosco School in Ngodi-Akwa used to call Mama Mbila. She smiled at the memory. She read the information, handwritten by a state official. Her surname, first name, place of birth, and above all, her date of birth—August 4, 1971, instead of August 4, 1976. She remembered Uncle Démoney ordering her to drum her new date of birth into her head: August 4, 1971. An extra five years! She heard Démoney's loud, authoritative voice saying, *Remember this! From now on, you were born on August 4, 1971. OK?* She saw herself again—so young, head hung low, powerless—simply answering, *Yes, Papa.*

Mbila wept.

Oyono moved closer and stroked her blond wig. He rested his hand on the nape of the young woman's neck to ease the pain tormenting her. He did his best to comfort her, but Mbila couldn't hold back her tears. She wept freely at flashbacks from those two years of forced prostitution. She remembered her first client, "good news" from Oyono. He'd been as hairy as a Bern bear and so fat that public health officials would have been appalled, his gigantic gut hiding a dick that was definitely too small. This "good news" had been so pot-bellied that Mbila had wondered what sort of acrobatics he needed to perform to get even a glimpse of the tip of his own foreskin. That man, her first client, had been revolting. He'd had bad breath, stinking armpits, a flaking, bald scalp, and dirty nails. An ogre. But he was Oyono Bivondo's "good news."

Mbila wept as she remembered the low points of her exploitation. She remembered how she'd suffered as depraved Turkish kebab sellers penetrated her in more than one place. She cried as she thought about the tough Blacks who'd paid a pittance to release their insatiable urges on her for days on end. She remembered the times she'd had to risk her own health, accepting requests from guys who paid well, fathers and always-on-a-business-trip husbands who shamelessly asked her to freefall without a parachute. Oh! Those bastards! She pitied their poor wives each time those guys collapsed on her, unconscious, balls completely empty. She also remembered the times she'd been afraid and even panicked when the Geneva police, prompted by outraged 1968 feminist politicians, patrolled the Pàquis looking to clean up the girls on sale. Periods of destitution flashed back, the low tides, as she called them, when days went by without a single man turning up to ask her to spread her legs. Times she thought she'd never manage to pay off her debt.

It all flooded back, and Mbila cried hard-hard, as though her tears could wash away the dirty memories forcing themselves on her, memories that were still under her skin, seared into her very being.

As my mother tells me about this part of her life, she begins to cry. I cry too. I can't control it. But I also start to feel a bit awkward. It's embarrassing to think that my mother had been a sex slave. Even though I love her, I would prefer her to be more traditional, simpler, without that kind of hou nson in her past.

She was free now. What was she going to do with her freedom? So long awaited, so long desired. Mbila quickly realized this freedom would just take her right back to square one, still illegal, still unable to meet even her most basic needs. She realized she still faced the eternal anguish of a life without papers—a forced return ready to ambush her wherever she went. She lamented her life of exploitation.

"Why are you crying?" Oyono asked.

"What am I going to do now? What am I going to do with this passport, eh?"

"But you're free now. You can do whatever you want with it."

"But I'm not free. This passport doesn't give me any rights. It doesn't give me the right to stay here. This isn't my country; you know that as well as I do. I used to be scared I'd be arrested by the police because I was an illegal prostitute. And I'll still be scared of getting arrested by the police because I'm still illegal. This passport is no use to me. It actually makes things worse! Now they can easily check my identity and put me on a plane quick-quick. Now I'll be both an illegal immigrant and homeless! I'm sure you and your guys won't waste any time taking back the little apartment you lent me on 39 rue de Berne. You'll put another girl in there. So tell me—what good is my freedom to me?"

"You're right," sighed Oyono before adding, "but I've got a solution, just for you."

"A solution? What sort of solution?" she asked.

"Mbila, I know you're a lot younger than this passport suggests. The Philanthropists told me everything on the phone not long ago. Your father sure took a lot of risks sending you here at such a young age. I'm also pleased to tell you that you've done what was expected of you. More, in fact. You made a huge profit. We've never had a girl as good as you before. Not a single client ever complained about you. You never betrayed us. So that's why I've got even more good news for you," declared Oyono.

"You and your good news."

"I'll use some of the profit you made to get you some papers. Don't ask me how it works; it's too hard to explain. All you need to know is that you'll start the procedure to get married tomorrow. You'll get married to one of our partners, Bertrand Rappard," continued Oyono.

"Married? Get married to someone I don't even know? That's your good news, is it?" Mbila challenged him. "I've never even met this Bertrand guy. I don't even know what he looks like. And you're asking me to marry him?"

"Oh, Mbila darling, it's so sweet that you're still so naive even after two years in Geneva! Look, it's called a sham marriage. This way you can marry someone who has papers, a Swiss guy, in this case, Geneva born and bred, and get a bona fide residence permit. It couldn't be easier!" explained Oyono.

"Really? You're telling the honest truth?" the young woman shouted, overjoyed.

"But why would I lie, Mbila? You're as free as a bird!" he announced.

Mbila suddenly felt light. So light she almost fell off her stool. Without thinking, she flung herself around his neck. His shoulder seemed to offer the comfort and assurance she needed. She shed a tear. But she immediately pulled herself together again. Should she really believe this feyman and his new kind of good news? Hadn't he been the cause of all the torture she'd been through? Despite all the terrible things that bastard Oyono had done to her, she was still under his spell. That's why she couldn't resist his advances. Blinded by his good looks, she followed him across the road and up to the fourth floor of 39 rue de Berne.

Their first encounter may not have produced any offspring, but this one did. My mother fell pregnant.

IX

I NEVER KNEW my father.

I had a mother, and that was more than enough for me. Anyway, most of my friends at school didn't have fathers either. So why worry? Blond Silvia and Brunette Romaine only had their mothers and their Barbie dolls. My Latino friend Saarinen only had his mum too, Belén. So the concept of fatherhood didn't really mean anything to me, other than being a rarity.

At the age of twenty-three—well, eighteen, actually—my mother was pregnant to Oyono Bivondo and married to Bertrand Rappard. That guy never even saw his sham wife while she was pregnant. He had just married her and collected his mbongo. And just like that, he became my father, like winning a prize at a funfair, without even knowing I existed. So that's why I'm called Dipita Rappard!

I never met my progenitor, Oyono. Well, once . . . but that's another story. I'll get to that later. And after everything Mama had told me about him, I have to admit I'd never really wanted to see him. I'd only ever despised him, even though there was a lovey-dovey hint of ndolo in Mama's eyes any time she talked about him. She seemed torn between love and hate, desire and repulsion. She was still under his spell, but I hated him without ever having met him.

As far as I was concerned, if I had to have a father, then it was my mother's sham husband, Bertrand Rappard. But this Mr. Rappard—I always called him Mr. with a certain sense of detachment—well, I only met him much later, when I was a teenager.

I was sixteen when my mother first introduced me to her ex-husband. I say ex-husband because they were no longer together; they hadn't been for a long time. Well, they'd never really been together. Officially, their marriage had lasted five years. They got divorced as soon as my mother became a Swiss citizen.

Deal done.

That was Mr. Rappard's business model: he received money (lots of money, my mother had explained) in exchange for sham marriages. That was the only thing Mr. Rappard contributed to his partnership with Oyono Bivondo, my biological father. All Mr. Rappard did was help get paperwork for girls who had been trafficked and exploited, girls who were known for being submissive and long-suffering. Don't go thinking the guy was an idiot, though. I reckon he was actually pretty smart! He always made sure to leave at least three years between marriages to avoid attracting attention from government officials, who really should have been asking a hundred questions about his life, like-like what he was doing spending all his time getting married, divorced, remarried, then divorced again. He hadn't worked a single day in his life apart from getting married; that was his profession—he was a marrier.

"Dipita! Dipita!" my mother had shouted at the top of her voice one day, like I was miles away.

I had jumped up from my Acer computer on the small desk in my room, the only place I could study when there was a bit of peace and quiet on rue de Berne. Our two-bedroom apartment with its tiny lounge was so cramped we would have easily heard even a cat's velvety paws padding through the kitchen from our bedrooms. It was the same when the neighbors did naughty things and when my mother was working. It felt like our old building was made of cardboard.

Just three steps and I was at the front door, right beside my mother. That's when I saw her with a man. Average build, a bit of a belly, but not too big, just a small paunch. He wore a light-blue checked shirt, jeans, a velvet jacket, and black loafers. Understated and elegant. And definitely well into his forties. A well-groomed mustache graced his upper lip but didn't hide it entirely. Short hair, graying at the temples, a bit like George Clooney. He was sexy. To be honest, he didn't look that bad compared to the strange guys who turned up at our door for another kind of appointment.

And he didn't look anything like the Blacks who showed up either. Always impeccably dressed, slightly mysterious, eyes well hidden behind huge shades even on the darkest winter nights, they'd lock themselves away with Mbila in her room for hours on end, talking.

"Dipita," said my mother, "I'd like to introduce you to Mr. Rappard."

"Hello, Mr. Rappard."

He held out his hand. I accepted his handshake. It was polite yet brief. Mbila invited us into the living room for a cup of tea.

I sat down on my pear-shaped pouf. I looked long and hard at this guy I'd heard her mention a few times. I wondered why he'd turned up at our place after such a long time. Was he going to ask Mbila for more money? Was he here to blackmail her? I paid close attention to his mannerisms and the way he spoke. Charlotte the hairdresser always says it's the little things that help you spot those bastard gigolos quick-quick. But after watching him, I thought he seemed pretty nice—maybe not wealthy, but financially stable. I thought it might not be such a bad idea for Mbila and me to reconnect with him. He could help my mother pay for my design course. He could help my comrade and uncle back home. Hadn't he helped Mbila stay in Switzerland? And what if he could get her out of prostitution? I thought. But if my mother gave up work, I risked losing all my jobs: PR manager, business associate, partner, and even psychologist! I started to worry about a guy like this coming back into our lives. But there was nothing to fear; that much I could see from the way Mbila the Bantu princess was acting, rocking gently in her chair as she smoked a joint.

The meeting was amicable. I didn't stay long before going back to my room, leaving my mother alone with her guest. I gave Mr. Rappard a quick wave to say bye. I never saw him again.

I grew up in my mother's exclusively female universe: stars, beauty, bling-bling, and above all, gossip. Oh, what a wonderful world! I loved it so much I gave up my dreams of becoming a banker like I'd promised my uncle. I wanted to study a subject generally assumed to be the preserve of the female sex—fashion. I wanted to become a dressmaker. My friend Saarinen used to correct me every time I used that word. He'd tell me to say designer, not dressmaker.

"You're not going to become a dressmaker, are you?" he'd object, looking at me like he felt that hou nson for me. "Little dressmaker sounds too much like a ditsy little lady around the corner who doesn't know what to do with her life apart from stab herself with her own pins and needles. Designer, you know, that's much more masculine, more ambitious, more sophisticated. Classy, even! Designer makes you think of Yves Saint Laurent, Giorgio Armani, and the rest of them. Totally different to the dressmaker down the road."

I was of exactly the same opinion, so I agreed: "Yes, Saarinen, you're right, I want to become a designer!"

A female universe. Only women. Beautiful women who, like my mother, dedicated themselves to their looks, their stunning wardrobes, their high heels, and their bespoke hairdos. Apart from the Nigerian hairdresser Charlotte, all the women who came to our apartment were wolowoss in and around rue de Berne. They worked in shifts, some in the morning, others in the afternoon and evening, and the rest at night. The shift pattern made sure they rotated. Each girl got at least one night a week, because that's when there were the most clients. All those shy, simple virgins, all those discreet married guys, all those men who want to do naughty things only come out after dark—they all descended on rue de Berne after midnight.

As a child, I used to watch the girls fight each other in the street from my bedroom window. One girl shouted in a thick Spanish accent, "Es mi cliente, I saw him first." Another girl, as dark skinned as she was wild, shouted back, "I don't care! You might have seen him first, but he chose me first. That's the difference, poor little chola!" Still arguing, the two women started tugging on the client. Overwhelmed, the guy sneaked slowly-slowly back into his car and disappeared before he attracted too much attention. Left behind, the two women went at it like cock and bull. I split my sides laughing. When I told my friends about it at school the next day, they didn't get it at all. They were snoring away soundly in their beds at nine o'clock every night. Their parents, or their mothers, to be precise, sent them to bed early. I, on the other hand, sometimes only went to bed at one or two in the morning.

To put an end to the big-big rivalry between the girls on rue de Berne, my mother and a few other more experienced girls decided to set up an association: Associated Women of the Pâquis, AP for short.

And of course, the AP headquarters were on the fourth floor of 39 rue de Berne. Mama and her friends would have preferred the prestigious Place des Nations quarter in Geneva, where the big UN building and lots of other international organizations are based. But that was beyond their wildest dreams. Their AP was just a simple association; it didn't even have any real rules of procedure. Charlotte was the impartial president. Belén was the main convener. Apart from that, the AP girls didn't really have any clear objectives beyond getting together from time to time for a drink and chat about what happened at work.

I knew all those beautiful women. They had all helped raise me in one way or another. I saw them all as mothers because back home in Cameroon, any woman who helps raise a child is its mother. What did it matter if my cousin Loudmouth Pitou got worked up about the difference between a progenitor and parent?

My mothers met regularly—very regularly, in fact—in our little lounge for a vodka, cup of black tea, wheat beer, fat joint, or slim cigarette. They chatted about all their wolowoss stuff. The older girls taught the younger ones how to escape police patrols and violent clients who were learned idiots. The bit I liked best was when they swapped sex tips: how to get a rough guy to come more slowly; how to make sure you douche properly, ready to satisfy guys who like using the back door; how to suck a dick so well the client ends up comatose; which positions increase the client's pleasure; how to and why you should avoid reaching orgasm with a client. It was all music to my little business partner–psychologist ears.

I spent a lot of time with my AP mothers, sitting there on my pear-shaped pouf, listening to their gossip and wolowoss business. When I wasn't with the prostitutes, I was with my friends who loved Barbies, of course, Blond Silviane and Brunette Romaine, and there was never a single naughty thought in my head. There were no men whatsoever in my world, apart from Saarinen.

X

FROM THE WINDOW of the cell I call my room, I contemplate the autumn colors sparkling like fireworks outside. Seasons change and leaves must fall, one by one, to gather on the damp ground. And that's what's happening now. Dead autumn leaves carpet the ground around the prison fortress and the concrete courtyard within. In the distance, the Champ-Dollon fields glow a dazzling array of reds, greens, and yellows. As I look out at the colorful cocktail, I sense a new glimmer of hope. Hope for change, hope for freedom, hope for a new life after prison.

A gentle breeze swirls the leaves lying orphaned on the gray concrete courtyard. I want to be swept away by the breeze. I want it to take me far, far, far away from where I am right now. I want this gentle breeze to transport me like a clando car and carry me all the way to Africa, to Cameroon, so I can see my uncle again and tell him that even though I did something terrible, I haven't really changed. I'm still his little Dipita, the little nkana he talked to like a son, a future heir. I want to tell him I'm his little nkana who probably won't become a banker anymore as we'd agreed, but a designer instead. And designer is just as impressive as banker, right?

I want to tell him I'm still his Dipita, his good little boy, the one he let in on his secret about his penniless bank. I'm the boy who'll never let a single secret escape in a burp from his belly. I want to tell him that I don't cry, that I never ever cry. That would be a lie, but that kind of lie is OK. Mama taught me that when I was her PR manager. So I'd tell my uncle I never cry, even though in other ways I've become *like that*, just like those men he didn't want me to become. I remember his words well-well. They still ring in my ears: *My son, never become like the white men who cry like women or do naughty things with other men like them.* I often think about what he said, about the very clear instructions that I ended up disobeying. Every time I remember his words, I feel a truckload of pain in my belly. I would have done anything to get *that* out of me, anything to please my uncle.

I want to tell him I haven't forgotten the most important thing—family. I want to tell him I often think about him; I think about Auntie who burns her fingers every morning frying accra banana. I think about my cousin Loudmouth Pitou too, even though he used to annoy me with all that stuff about deviant behavior. I want to tell him I think about them all, constantly, every day.

I want to say all of this to my uncle, to regain his trust and be given a second chance. Isn't that what our prison supervisor keeps saying? Doing time in prison isn't the end of the world. So why shouldn't I be able to start again from scratch and keep my promise to help my family in Africa?

From my room, I watch the birds fly across the sunny sky on this mild autumn day. I want to ask them to pass on my message to my beloved uncle thousands of miles away. I want to talk to the sun god like my uncle did so well. I want to ask the sun god to help me. So I close my eyes and send up a prayer to him. "Oh heavenly god! Oh divine star! Oh god of my uncle! Grant me the courage to serve my sentence in serenity. Grant me the courage to imagine a future that is a little brighter. Oh heavenly god! Oh divine star! Oh god of my uncle! Do not shut your ears to my requests."

After this short prayer, I clench my jaw tight-tight to stop even the tiniest tear from escaping. No, I don't want to cry. Right now, I need to keep that promise, at least—to never cry. Never cry like those white men . . . but it's impossible. I can't control it. I cry my heart out.

And to dry my tears, I send my spirit soaring. I gaze out on the gray prison courtyard. I see the patch of grass in the middle. The drab Champ-Dollon Prison courtyard contrasts starkly with the bright autumn colors beyond. The wind picks up again, making the dead leaves whirl. I imagine I'm those leaves, light, oh so light, carried, carried away by the wind . . .

~

One evening when I was studying, eyes glued to my old Acer computer screen, my mother came into my tiny bedroom, stirring a Maggi stock cube in a jug.

"Everything OK, sweetheart?"

I smiled at her. She came over and tried to read a few words on the slides I was studying. With a bit of effort, she managed to read the title: "The e-las-tic-i-ty of de-mand in re-la-tion to price. Ooooooh my little boy Dipita!" she shouted, clapping. "You're doing those complicated white people things now. Elasticity this, elasticity that."

"Come on, stop it! It's not a white people thing. The elasticity of demand in relation to price is just the variation in demand in relation to the price—" I tried to explain.

"No! No! No! Don't talk to me about all that white people stuff," she said, brushing me off.

"No, really! It's not complicated. It's pretty simple, actually. It can help you understand a few things about your work," I replied.

"Oh, really?" she asked.

"If you raise your prices, you'll lose a lot of clients, and if you drop your prices, then all the men will come to you and not go to the other girls. That's all!" I concluded.

"That's it? But I already knew all that. White people sure like to complicate simple things with big-big words. Elasticity this, elasticity that. Do they want to make us all elastic or what? I can tell you one thing, Dipita. I'll never drop my prices. Quite the opposite, in fact—I'll keep putting them up, because clients won't think I'm high-class if I drop my prices. You get it?"

"Exactly! You're luxury goods, Mama!" I agreed.

"Wow, Dipita! You're saying I'm a luxury product, like a Gucci or Yves Saint Laurent dress?" my mother asked.

"Exactly."

"Me, Mbila, a luxury product! Oh, I'll have to tell all the girls tomorrow night when we open our AP meeting," she said excitedly.

My mother did a few Bikutsi steps as she stirred her Maggi stock cube. I laughed. We were interrupted by a soft, husky voice.

"Well, well, Auntie Mbila, you never told me you were such a good dancer."

I looked toward the door and saw a tall young man with blond hair, bright-blue eyes, plump lips, and magnificently sculpted broad shoulders. Oh my accra banana! My heart skipped a beat and then started pounding so hard I thought it was doing a Bi-ZiZi dance. I'd never seen such a good-looking guy in my life. I'd just been struck by love at first sight.

My mother stopped dancing. She readjusted her miniskirt, cleared her throat, and said, "Honestly, Dipita, you've got me all worked up with your talk of elastic and luxury brands. Come on; let me introduce you to William. He's Mr. Rappard's son." Then she turned to the good-looking blond and said, "William, this is Dipita, my son."

So Mr. Rappard had a son? Until then, I was sure the only thing that guy did was get married and divorced, nothing else. With whom could he have had such a handsome son? Was he William's biological father or adoptive father, like he was for me? So I had a brother? A totally blond white brother?

William held out his hand. I held out mine, quivering and clammy.

"Hi, Dipita," he said, smiling.

"He-e-llo, Wi-lli-am," I stammered, completely blown away by how handsome he was.

"William was bored at his mum's; she's a cota in Bernex. So I suggested he spend the night at our place with you. I'm sure you'll get on like a house on fire. Gotta dash, sorry. I have to go to work. I'm staying at Charlotte's tonight; she's away and asked me to liven up her apartment a bit. So I'll be at her place. You'll have peace to study elastic and luxury goods without me disturbing you with my clients. Well then, boys, I'm off. Don't do anything I wouldn't."

And my mother disappeared just like that, leaving me with my brother, a guy who made me swoon. I felt like shouting out to Mbila, "Nooooo! Don't leave me here with him! Please don't leave us alone! Noooo!" But she was already out chasing clients on rue de Berne. And I was left there, face-to-face with William.

He seemed much more relaxed than me. He wouldn't stop smiling; maybe he thought it would help me relax, feel less stressed. But it had exactly the opposite effect. It just poured more oil on the fire of my heart, which was already burning bright. What could I say? How could I break the ice? How could I talk to him without accidently belching out even the tiniest hint of how he made me feel? Mention our unlikely family connection? That would be far too personal an opener. Talk about my mother's work? Maybe, but not with a stranger. The only thing I could do was pull some drawers over my mouth.

"Your mum says you're studying elastic and luxury brands, right?" he asked, probably as a way of breaking the ice gently.

"No. It wasn't elastic and luxury brands. I was just explaining the concept of elasticity of demand in relation to price," I replied.

"Oh. Well, that's entirely different," he said.

"Yeah. You know it?" I asked.

"Of course. Of course I know it. I'm studying for my business diploma. I'm learning about basic economics right now too," he explained.

"How old are you?" I asked.

"I'm eighteen—you?"

"Seventeen," I replied.

William didn't reply. I went back to my computer, pretending to concentrate, but my head was buzzing. William took a good look around my room. He scanned the walls and found a new topic of conversation—my sketches.

"Did you draw those?" he asked.

"Yes."

"Wow, they're great!" he said admiringly.

"Thanks."

"I'd never be able to draw such gorgeous dresses on models. If you keep it up, you'll become a famous dressmaker," he suggested.

"Not a dressmaker, a designer," I replied.

"OK, designer then. You could be like Yves Saint Laurent and make loads of money," he continued.

"Hmmmm."

"Remember me when you're famous. With my business diploma, I'll be able to help you with sales and marketing," William concluded.

"OK," I agreed.

I didn't say a word. I didn't budge from my swivel chair. Only the sun god knew what was coursing through my body. It was like a merry-go-round of emotions: fear, shame, anxiety, desire, pain, and of course ndolo, love.

William complained that it was too hot in our tiny apartment. All of a sudden, he unbuttoned his short-sleeved shirt and lay down on my bed. *Grrr! Grrr!* I ordered my eyes to stay glued to my computer screen, but they obstinately disobeyed me and began to inspect the well-toned abs of the guy beside me, the guy in my room, on poor little Dipita's bed. William had a body like the cement block makers', like Auntie Bilolo's assos. Perfectly sculpted, a six-pack like the ones I saw every morning on the shopping channel. William could have been a model from one of those shows that remind you early-early in the morning that you must consume to exist. A simple mantra—I consume, therefore I am.

"Hmmmm, Wi-ll-i-am, do you want a cup of tea?"

"Yes please," he replied enthusiastically. He was probably pleased to hear me speak again, finally. He must have been overjoyed to hear me ask him a question, to see me voluntarily offer myself at his service. I was happy too, of course, but for a different reason—I could finally escape him for a few seconds. Phew! By fleeing to the kitchen, I'd have a chance get my heart to stop racing and beg the sun god, Allah, Jesus and the Virgin Mary, and even Buddha himself to help me breathe with a little more Zen. Just a teeny, tiny bit of Zen.

What a task it was to make that tea! Real torture! I was shaking like a leaf. I burned my fingers a million times. I yelped so many times that William got worried and asked, "Are you OK, Dipita?"

I replied, "Yes, everything's fine! Don't worry!"

To cool off a bit, I opened the kitchen window and stuck my head out into the racket of rue de Berne. Cars fought for space in the narrow street; some were even on the sidewalk. *Beep! Beep! Beep! Out of my way, bastard! But this is the sidewalk, idiot!* Horns honked, making the already noisy street pulsate even more. The kebab shops grilled pork to satisfy customers who were as hungry as they were stupid. The tiny shops run by Sri Lankans kept the alcohol flowing endlessly, despite the prohibition of sales after 9:00 p.m. *Huh? Who cares!* The bars welcomed their clientele, a mix of well-heeled tyrants, noses in the air, and down-and-out liars without a single mbongo to their name. A line of North Africans set their lungs on fire, holding their cigarettes or fat joints between thumb and index finger to look more manly, more virile. Glum-looking men and women waited at laundromats. And the drug dealers, o! I almost forgot to mention those guys. They sized up their customers like wild animals watching prey. And, of course, there were the wolowoss, tottering on their high-high Lady Gaga heels or sitting on stools, waiting patiently-patiently for their tricks. Looking down on all the hustle and bustle of the place where I'd grown up happy, I was able to catch my breath again. I was able to breathe normally. There I was, like a little goldfish in its bowl. I was in my natural habitat, my ecosystem, rue de Berne. But for how much longer?

I went back to the two cups of tea I'd had so much trouble making, which were starting to get cold. I picked them up, took a deep breath, and prepared to head back to my room where I would have to face William and his charms. I hadn't even moved when he appeared at the kitchen door, smiling, holding my computer, and asked, "Hey, Dipita, are you gay?"

Some questions catch you off guard, a bit like Uncle Démoney's ndongo ndongo landing on top of your head. *Whack! Whack!* Confused and bewildered, I dropped the two teacups. They smashed to smithereens. A shard of porcelain grazed my right foot.

"Ouch!"

"Are you OK, Dipita?"

"Yes, I'm fine! Don't worry!" Liar!

How the hell had I forgotten about the Gay Romeo profile I'd left open on my laptop? Only a huge burqa could have hidden the hou nson showering my entire body right then.

Gay Romeo is an online dating site for men. I spent a lot of time on it chatting with a few faggots in my area, as well as farther afield in Switzerland and neighboring France. It was a way to socialize, virtually at least, with other guys *like that*, like me. It helped me feel like I wasn't the only person in the world who was so different from everyone else. I still remembered Uncle Démoney's words: *Son, never become like those white men.* But even Uncle's harsh-harsh words hadn't stopped me from hanging around on that site, a place I liked to call the Meat Market. I thought it was a good name because there were all sorts of guys there: skinny, fat, pigs, young, old, walking corpses, cute, ugly, monsters, ready-made, and past their sell-by date.

Uncle's words had been so harsh and had made me feel so isolated that I'd felt less alone when I discovered the Meat Market—finally. And even less so when I realized that a lot of tough Pâquis machos roamed the Meat Market too, guys I saw hanging around my street every day.

Less isolated, I felt confident, at home, protected by the secrecy of our virtual world, and gradually realized with pride that perhaps I wasn't as strange-strange as Uncle thought.

I enjoyed chatting day in, day out at the Meat Market. I improved my faggot lingo: hookup for casual sex—WH for well hung, T for top, B for bottom, S for submissive, BBK for bare backing (you know, raw dogging), sneakers for guys who liked to sniff dirty socks, pics for photos, and so on.

Conversations at the Meat Market were short and sweet: *hi! hi! how r u? good and u? good, what u looking 4? bit of everything ☺, and u? a hookup. cool, u hung? yes & u? normal. u top or bottom?*

I never acted on any of it. I was too scared to because I wasn't supposed to be on that sort of website. I was only seventeen. Keen to keep a low profile, I never went any further than chatting, never revealed my real identity or showed my face. I didn't have any pictures on my profile.

I remembered my invisible friend from the Meat Market. His login was YoungNCute, mine was CuriousDude. I shared a lot with YoungNCute. We talked about high school, our annoying teachers, our dreams for the future, how much we wanted to find true love, our absent parents (but never their jobs). We talked about our morning urges to do those-those things, our red-light dreams, our night-time defilements, jerking off in the shower, our fear of anal sex.

But despite all that, I'd never sent YoungNCute a facepic. He hadn't sent one either. We were friends, lovers even, without ever having met. That's what I loved about the Meat Market, the chance to share my fears, joys, and desires with others without ever having to reveal myself.

I thought about YoungNCute all the time, my imaginary lover. In my mind he was young and cute, just like his login. I imagined him exactly like the info on his profile: 1.87 meters, 80 kilos Caucasian, well-toned. Sometimes I wondered if YoungNCute really was young and cute. Maybe he was just an old guy chasing younger men. But deep down, I knew there was a truckload of ndolo in my belly for YoungNCute.

My profile was still open, along with the PowerPoint from my course, and my Facebook account too, of course. My motto was "remain sociable, even when studying." But it had just backfired and given away my secret about *that thing* to William.

I went back to my room to tend to my small wound while William stayed in the kitchen to mop up the tea I had spilled. He came back into my room a few minutes later. Attentive, he sat down beside me, placed one hand on my shoulder, and asked how I was.

"Are you OK, Dipita?"

I just spat back the same answer: "Yes, I'm fine! Don't worry!" Oh, what a liar I was!

"I'm sorry if I offended you. I shouldn't have gone anywhere near your computer."

"Oh, don't worry—no need to apologize," I replied curtly.

"I just wanted to play a video game, wait patiently, you know."

"No worries. It's fine."

Silence again. I decided to leave my cut for now to avoid having to face William. He still had his hand on my shoulder. I was melting like butter in a hot pan. I held my breath so I wouldn't blurt out a thing. But all my heart could do was leap-leap. Oh, how I would have liked to use my uncle's ndongo ndongo to call it back to order.

"You know, YoungNCute, that's me," William whispered.

What do you say when you find yourself face-to-face with your secret fantasy? I didn't believe him. It was too good to be true. It had to be a joke. What if it was true? I wondered. My lower lip trembled feverishly. Had Mama set me up? It would have been too easy to believe in a conspiracy theory. But what could I say after a revelation like that? Tell him that's what I'd thought? Tell him I'd known? Too easy, right? Tell him he'd got it wrong? Maybe. And even if he was wrong, how did he know I'd been chatting to someone called YoungNCute at the Meat Market? Had he found out by poking his nose into my account? Yes, probably. But let's not think about that—the most important thing about this revelation was that he was *like that* too!

I slowly lifted my head and looked at him; his hand was still on my shoulder.

"So you're YoungNCute?"

William simply nodded in response. He took his hand off my shoulder. He gazed into space. What was he looking at? I didn't have a clue. My sketches on the walls? My Acer computer? The tiny cut I didn't really want to deal with? Pretending I needed some air, I inched away from him as we sat there on my bed. "It's hot-hot in here," I managed to say. William took my hand. What did that mean? Where were the AP girls when I needed them to tell me what to do in this sort of situation? Apparently this wasn't a joke. There was something to it. I was living out my dream. I moved closer to William. I looked up and caught his eye. I touched his face. Our lips met automatically, as though swept along by a kind of grace. We kissed tenderly, passionately, wildly. I devoured him and he devoured me. He quickly dropped his pants and I saw underpants stretched-stretched by his *thing*. It was as straight and sweet as the plantains Auntie Bilolo used to make her special accra banana.

YoungNCute, o! William certainly had something to be proud of down there. In faggot lingo you'd say he was hung like a horse. I touched his *thing* as he undressed me quick-quick. He placed his hands on my shoulders and pushed me to my knees. I hesitated briefly, thinking about Uncle Démoney and his advice. I got the horrible feeling I was a traitor. A faint sense of self-condemnation rose up within me. I also thought of my mother, a wolowoss, a whore, and those men who entered her bedroom every night. I thought of my mother in that submissive position in front of those engorged *things*, kneeling for an insistent or even violent client. I hated those men, hated their dicks, hated my sexuality. I thought about saying no. The feeling was so strong, I wanted to bite down hard on that erection right there in my face, just waiting for my tongue. But the desire surging up from deep-deep within me overwhelmed that budding loathing. "Father," I heard myself say, "forgive me, for I know not what I'm doing." Unconsciously, automatically, I opened my mouth wide. William filled it with his plantain, and I got an aftertaste of Auntie Bilolo's accra banana.

William, a.k.a. YoungNCute, placed his hands on my head as though to bless me, baptize me—amen. I decided to focus on what was most salient, closing my eyes and allowing myself to be carried away by my desire on the one hand and my reluctance on the other. All those little tips shared in a spirit of solidarity at the AP meetings flooded back: where to place your tongue; how to open your mouth so you don't choke; how to produce as much saliva as possible to better swallow his knob. Oh, I remembered, almost proud of myself, that Charlotte the hairdresser always said the main thing, the most important thing, in fact, was to remember the balls! William groaned like a trapped animal as I licked his. Without warning, he grabbed me and threw me onto my narrow bed. Ass up, I didn't have time to ask him to wait until I'd douched like one of the girls at the AP had recommended. Standing behind me, built like an athlete, he gently lifted my hips toward him and . . . bingo, that was it.

I let out a cry like a Zulu warrior. Why did I scream? Was it because it hurt? Because I thought I was turning into a wolowoss like the AP girls? Because my mind was replaying Uncle Démoney, his ndongo ndongo hanging from his mouth, telling me that what I was doing was evil? Perhaps I screamed for all those reasons at the same time. What do I know—I just screamed, that's all. That's why William covered my mouth with one of his strong hands. I felt degraded, silenced, humiliated. Episodes from my mother's dark past flashed before my eyes. I wanted to pull myself together, rebel, shout even louder than the street hawkers in the Ngodi-Akwa market. But my body gave in, weak. William curved against my back, and I felt his warmth penetrate me. "Sssssh! Relax," he said. I buttoned my lip and relaxed.

XI

"SO TELL ME—how's it going with your sweetheart?" hairdresser Charlotte asked while the rest of the AP girls split their sides laughing.

I hadn't expected a question like that. How did she know I had a guy? How was she so certain? But her street hawker's stare was sure-sure.

"I've got no idea what you're talking about, Mama Charlotte," I replied.

The girls burst out laughing again, and I started to feel uncomfortable. They were so sure of their information that they weren't going to be deterred with an evasive answer and attempt to play it cool.

"Come on, son," continued Charlotte, the leader of the pack. "I didn't drop down from the sky yesterday. And all that cutesy Chéri Coco couple stuff, I've already seen it all."

"Oh, Charlotte, leave our little baby alone," interrupted Belén, Saarinen's mother and the main convener of the AP.

Belén was Bolivian. Her physique was pretty much what you'd expect in a wolowoss. Her pointy-pointy chest could have really hurt someone. She was always keen to show it off, squeezing it into a bra or corset a good few sizes too small.

The other AP girls agreed with Bélen. "Belén's right," said Maïmouna, a wasp-waisted Rwandan addicted to black lipliner.

"Belén's right," chimed in Tran-Hui, a Thai woman whose body was as tiny as her face. "Either you get to the point, or you leave our darling Dipita in peace."

"It's always like this in this association. You never let me finish. You always interrupt me," moaned Charlotte.

A long, disapproving *oooh* rose up, filling the air with toxic nicotine. "Go on then, Charlotte! Talk!" shouted the other AP girls.

"Out with it, Charlotte. We just want a bit of paz," declared Belén. Charlotte was pleased with this vote of confidence. Just as they were acting like children in a playground, William walked in. He was carrying a tray with a few cups, sugar, and my mother's oriental teapot, a gift from Tran-Hui, the Thai woman. But what the hell was he doing there? He hadn't told me he was coming to call.

William carefully placed the tray on the small table in our cramped lounge. He sat down on the mat on the floor beside Mbila. All the girls smiled at him, then turned in unison to look at me with the same knowing smile. It was too weird to be true. What if I'd got it all wrong? What if William wasn't Mr. Rappard's real-real son? And what if it was actually a huge trap set by the AP girls? To get me to belch out all the secrets I'd hidden down-down in my belly?

Charlotte carefully lowered her derriere into my mother's rocking chair. She cleared her throat like an African village chief and began to speak.

"Well, well. So, son. We know you are homosexual. No need to deny it because William already confessed everything to your mother, who then told us."

"Oh, so you set a trap for me. That's what happened, right?"

"What do you mean?" said Charlotte, surprised.

Her street-hawker stare turned sad, innocent. "Oh, Dipita, son, we'd never set you up. And definitely not for something like this," she said, raising three fingers, scout's honor.

I wanted to plonk my backside down somewhere. I scanned the room for my pear-shaped pouf so I could sink into it, the way I did at all the other AP meetings. Maybe it would know how to comfort me. Maybe it would know how to hide that hou nson I was feeling. I wanted to get out of that room, escape, flee, leave them to their opinions. But that would be too cowardly. And the respect I had for my mothers simply wouldn't let me. The only thing left to do was to stop holding my breath and sit down.

Charlotte took the floor again. "Darling, you can trust me. There's no conspiracy. Your mother saw you last night, you and William—"

"So what?" I snapped. "William, what's going on here? Come on, tell me! And what the heck are you doing here anyway?"

"Calm down. Take it easy, son," interrupted Mbila.

"You saw us naked in my bed; so what? What's the problem?"

No reply.

"Yes, I'm a faggot! Yes, I fucked him! Yes! That's what you want to hear, right? Well there you go! You heard it!"

A heavy silence settled in the room. It was the first time I'd ever raised my voice to my mothers. I began to cry. Ashamed, I wanted to escape to my room, but Charlotte's voice stopped me in my tracks.

"Don't cry, son. There's no need to get upset. It's all out in the open now, and I'd just like to conclude the matter by saying that you are free to be yourself. We aren't judging you, and we never will. You can always count on us to have your back, whether that's here in the Pâquis or somewhere else."

Her kind words were touching. I felt the anger that had been welling up within me vanish. I blushed with all the emotion. I broke down in tears again. I cried like a little child. I cried the way

Uncle had told me not to. William got up and came to my rescue. He held me and rubbed my back. I felt loved.

I'd always known that one day my mothers would accept me as I was. But I hadn't expected them to accept me so enthusiastically and with such kind words. After all, some of my mothers came from countries where people *like that* aren't exactly loved. Mbila, for example, was from Cameroon, where suspected faggots are locked up. Charlotte was from Nigeria, where they are happily stoned.

Amid this mishmash of emotions and warm embraces, I kept an eye on my own mother. Like her fellow AP sisters, she was swept up in the jubilation fanning strong-strong in our living room. With her radiant smile, she looked like she was as happy as a mother who had just heard her son had graduated from the University of Geneva, been hired by a big multinational in the Nations district, or was going to marry a sweet, beautiful woman and have a village of children. Mbila looked as happy as a mother whose son had been raised up by the political and administrative authorities.

But looking back, I wonder why Mama was so happy. Why such joy for ndolo between two guys? What was so joyful or joyous about it that made you celebrate like that? Then I remembered what Auntie always said: in times of joy, it's hard-hard to show the truckload of anger in your belly. That's why I thought my mother's joy might have been hiding some sort of sadness she couldn't express under the circumstances.

Wasn't Mbila like any other mother? Didn't she want grandchildren too? A woman who had suffered so much because she'd been made to appear older, trafficked, and sexually exploited—didn't she want offspring as a sign of her victory over the human foolishness to which she had fallen victim? She was raised by Auntie Bilolo in our traditions and culture; didn't she want to pass on this knowledge to a daughter-in-law? So why wasn't she showing any signs of disapproval? Or, at the very least, disappointment, distress, confusion, or embarrassment? Why didn't she even look slightly uncomfortable? But there was nothing. She honestly seemed proud of me. She seemed proud to have a son *like that*. Her teary eyes sparkled, and I could see that she didn't care what anyone else would say. She didn't give a damn about gossip. She didn't give a damn about people who would spread the message that her son had turned out like that—yes, *like that*—because of her. She didn't give a damn about anyone who would stretch-stretch their tongue like chewing gum and tell everyone else her son had been raised like a girl—as if there were different ways to raise girls and boys. No, Mbila seemed to piss on all that. She was proud: proud to be my mother, proud to be the mother of her only son. Faggot or not, I was still her loyal associate.

The festive atmosphere in the room didn't leave me cold, but I still wasn't completely swept up in their ululations. In fact, throughout my teens, I'd read so many coming-out stories that had turned sour, ending in fights, family breakdowns, rejections, and even suicide, that I was actually a bit sad things had turned out so well for me. I'd internalized those dark stories so well that it felt strange to be accepted so naturally by my mothers. Why was I so fortunate? My heart flipped between joy and resentment. Mostly resentment. I felt resentful because I wasn't being punished for my *thing*. I felt like I was betraying the teenagers whose sad stories I had soaked up on online forums. I thought it was a pity my experience wasn't like theirs. I wanted to suffer the rejection and torture of being excluded by my family, friends, and everyone else around me. I wanted to know what it was like to contemplate suicide, stage my death, picture it, and even have the courage to go through with it.

To me, coming out went hand in hand with suicide. I'd need to prepare everything carefully before belching it all out. For example, I thought you had to collect a ton of pills and ideally wash them down with plenty of alcohol. I wasn't so sure about an overdose, so I had planned to use a gun, the one from my military service, perhaps. A few bullets to the head would clear my mind in a flash. But the catch was that I couldn't picture myself playing the recruit in an army camp. I had always thought I'd take my own life before going there. It wasn't really my thing. So what was the best way to quietly end it all after coming out? A rope? Yes, a rope, that's it, I would think as I lay on my bed. A rope and a chair. I had often pictured myself, neck crooked, hanging from a rope tied to the bronze chandelier in our lounge. But when I imagined the look on my mother's face as she made the grisly discovery, my body dangling from a rope like tinsel on a Christmas tree, I thought I'd better find another way. Stop eating maybe? Lose weight and become anorexic? But anorexia's for girls, I thought.

So I came up with several scenarios: drown myself in Lake Geneva, throw myself under a train, jump out in front of a car on the motorway, to mention a few. In the depths of my despair, I considered all those options. But above all, I told myself I had to leave something behind before going. A note, for example. I wanted to copy my idol, Dalida. I wanted to write a farewell letter to tell my mother—no, my mothers—how much I loved them. I wanted to tell them it was because I loved them that I wanted to die and leave them in peace.

I'd actually already written my letter. I wanted to leave it as a Microsoft Word file on my Acer computer. But I gave up on that idea because I knew my mother would never find it—she doesn't know how to use a computer. So I'd taken a blank page and written, *Forgive me; I can't bear the thought of life as a faggot.* I had folded the page in four and hidden it well-well under my bed, patiently waiting for D-day.

But that morning, when I heard my mother and her AP girl-friends laughing like that, I felt ashamed. All my plans fell apart.

I really wanted to experience some sort of earth-shattering whirlwind so I'd have something shocking to post on a forum, some sort of pain I could share with others. For me, that would have been the best way to not only fight alongside those who were being persecuted but also, and above all, to exist. Yes, exist. Because I truly believed that to exist with my *thing*, I needed a story to tell. And an experience that was as rosy, plain sailing, and pain-free as what my mother and the AP girls were offering seemed so dull that I was actually disappointed.

XII

FROM THE VERY START, I'd been intrigued by my mother's secret rendezvous with those Black guys who acted strange and always hid-hid their eyes behind huge shades. They'd been coming to our place pretty much every month for nearly five years to spend hours talk-talking in Mama's bedroom.

One evening, after a long video call with William—we'd moved from the Meat Market to Skype—I snuggled up in bed. Unable to sleep, I thought about how blessed I was to have mothers like mine. I remembered the farewell note still slumbering beneath my mattress and realized it no longer had a purpose. I leaped out of bed, lifted the mattress, and extracted the sheet of paper. I couldn't bring myself to open it and read it. But I still remembered the words I'd written. I felt a slight pang of regret. I tore it to shreds and threw it in the trashcan. A truckload of happiness settled deep down within me and slowly spread through the rest of my body.

I could hear Mbila in her room next door. It was almost midnight, and she was getting ready to head out into the street. She was making so much noise with the hairdryer, makeup boxes, and clickety-clacking high heels that I couldn't relax.

My mother was taking longer than usual. So long that I even considered asking her to go off to work and leave me in peace. Just as I was thinking that, I heard her stride down the hall toward my bedroom. She burst in like a madwoman. She was in a total panic.

"Dipita, Dipita, I really need your help."

It wasn't the first time my mother had said that. Any time she couldn't decide which dress to wear or which high heels to totter on, she'd run to my room and say, *Dipita, Dipita, I really need you*. But her voice sounded different that night. Odd, anxious somehow. Why was Mbila so worked up if she was just getting ready to go out and catch some big game on rue de Berne as usual? Wasn't she a luxury brand? So why was she so worried?

"No, Mama, I really can't help you tonight. Just wear that black polyester dress we picked out last week. It helped you get a lot of clients last time, didn't it?"

"What on earth are you talking about? Can't you see I'm already dressed? Stop lazing around and come help me. It's an emergency!"

"An emergency?"

"Yes, come with me right now. We don't have any time to waste."

Caught off guard by my mother's insistence, I leaped up like a soldier unexpectedly called to the front line. There wasn't a second to waste. If my mother was in a state like that, then it really was an emergency because it wasn't like her to get work-worked up for no reason. I put on my slippers and followed her to her bedroom.

"What's so urgent?"

Ignoring my question, Mbila lifted the blanket on her bed. That's when I saw a few small white pellets carefully squashed into the shape of suppositories and wrapped in a transparent film a bit like the stuff you use in the kitchen. All in all, there were ten pellets the size of my little finger.

You didn't have to be an expert to realize what they were: drugs, coke to be precise. Oh lord, so Mama was also a drug mule!

"What's that, Mama? Dru—"

"Ssssssh!" she said, bringing her finger to her lips and glancing around like she was worried someone might be spying on us.

"But Mama, since when have you—"

"Ssssssh," she interrupted me again before whispering nervously, "This isn't the time for questions. Just help me. Help your poor mother out. I need you. Listen, I've already swallowed twenty. There's ten in my vagina, and another fifteen up my ass. I don't have enough space for these ten. You have to help me, please. Just do what I ask. It's easy; you'll see. And above all, no questions. Got it? No questions!"

Only the sun god knew what sort of truck was tearing my insides apart right then. Anguish? Hate? Anger? Fear? Disgust? Yes, disgust. Yes, that was it. Disgust. I'd never ever been disgusted at my mother. But that night, it felt like I was standing in front of a pile of shit. Shit, my mother. That's all I could see before me. How could I refuse? How could I ask her not to involve me in her schemes?

I grew up on rue de Berne, in the Pâquis neighborhood. I'd often heard about drug runners, police officers who occasionally reeled in a few big fish from international drug trafficking networks, and above all, small-time dealers who survived by selling laughable quantities. I'd read in gossip columns that, in the name of gender equality, there were even a few women in powerful positions in those Mafia networks. I knew some of them hid kilos of white powder in their gut before handing it over to the guys in charge. I'd heard a lot about it. The AP girls talked about it too. But I'd never imagined my mother could be involved in that kind of thing. I'd never imagined she could be in so deep she'd be brazen enough to drag me into it with her.

I thought I was dreaming. This wasn't my sweet, beautiful mother standing there in front of me; it was a wild savage. Her furrowed brow showed just how furious she was. Snorting like a bull at the sight of a blood-red rag, she looked like a madwoman. I had the feeling she'd do me in if I didn't comply. I had to obey her immediately because her look said *do what I tell you or you've had it*. I had to choose between my life and my mother's.

Along with the fear and truckload of disgust in my belly, there was now a truckload of confusion. Somewhere deep down, the desire to help my mother began to flicker too. But those good intentions were soon overshadowed by the thought of getting caught. According to the gossip columns, my main source of information, the police showed no mercy in cases like this. Zero tolerance, zilch! Depressing images flashed before me. I saw myself being taken away by tetchy police officers: handcuffed, dragged into court, chucked in prison for years.

After all, this was my mother. She was the one right there in front of me—a she-devil, red like Lucifer. My head was spinning; I was so confused. I thought I was about to pass out, but I needed to be more alert than ever. Precision, composure, and a cool head were required to do what Mama was asking. "Relax, Dipita. Relax. It's no big deal," I heard myself stutter.

"It's not hard. You're a beginner, so you can just swallow five of these pellets. Take them like normal tablets. Just make sure you don't drink too much water, or you might explode. You can carry five in your stomach and put the other five up your ass. At least there's one thing a gay son's good for!"

I was sickened. I couldn't believe it. It hurt, hearing those words come out of my mother's mouth. Sickening. How could she have been so tolerant when I came out and then say something like that? Sickening. Had she only supported me because she saw me, her sodomite son, as the perfect place to stash cocaine pellets? I was furious. So furious I was livid. I glared at my mother, fuming. If my respect for her hadn't been unconditional, I'd have spat in her face. A face I no longer recognized, it was so swollen, so strange. Huge beads of sweat dripped from her bulging, badly made-up brow. Her nostrils flared like a bull ready for a corrida. A fine line of clear mucus trickled from her nostrils. She wiped it away with the back of her hand. She was unrecognizable. She was controlled by some sort of spirit, possessed.

She gave me half a glass of water and urged me to swallow the cocaine pellets. "Go on, drink," she said. Shot through with fear and anger, I managed to swallow the big-big tablets.

Once I'd ingested the cocaine pellets, my mother grabbed me with both hands. She pulled down my pajamas and threw me onto her bed like a tiny pebble. Fear had made me as light as a feather. Terrified, I was ashen, weakened. Yet I wanted to fight back, object, cry for help, pray to the sun god to get me out of this shit. But I felt so weak, so powerless.

She didn't have any time to waste persuading me to put the rest of the suppositories containing white powder up my ass.

She puffed the snot out of her nose. I clenched my buttocks to keep them shut, so she tapped them: *spank, spank.* I clenched them even tighter. Dismayed, she gave me two hard smacks. The pain made me relax my innocent buttocks for a moment, letting her spread them like I was a sick baby, and *ptooey*—she spat into the crack. I immediately felt the first pellet make its way in, slowly but firmly. Then a second one, a third one, and the five pellets ended up inside me like a miniature rosary. Revolted and sullied, I began to cry. Tears flooded down my face. I languished with rage. The angrier I became, the weaker I felt. Weak, violated. Yes, that's the word. I felt like I'd been violated by my mother.

The farewell note I'd just torn up suddenly flashed before my eyes again. I regretted throwing it away so soon. It would no doubt have been useful after this humiliation. The emptiness I felt inside made me consider taking my life again. Leaving it all behind seemed a thousand times more appealing than the thought of facing my mother in the light of day the next morning.

"Stop crying and get up," Mbila growled through her clenched teeth.

As I lay on her bed, paralyzed by rage and sobbing, my mother's stern look ordered me to zip it. She ran to my room and returned with a black suit and white shirt. It was one of the outfits I wore on important occasions: weddings, birthdays, baptisms and the like. When I saw her with those clothes I was as stunned as a June bug. She thought my trials that evening were like a big occasion? I clenched my fists to control my anger. Without batting an eyelid, I pulled on the clothes she threw at me. She kept at me: "Hurry up! We don't have a lot of time. It's almost half past twelve. We're late. Stop crying. Be strong. Man up. I know plenty of faggots like you who do this! It doesn't kill them. And it won't take long. The drop-off isn't far. Sometimes I have to sit on trains for hours with these pellets. Get it? And it hasn't killed me yet. So be a good boy and walk normally. We only have to go a few hundred meters. It's not far."

"Where are we going?" I managed to stutter, in between hiccups of disgust.

"It's not far. And no more questions. Come on."

My mother dragged me by the hand like a little kid refusing to go to school on the first day of term. We took the stairs four at a time. In the hall, my mother turned and looked me straight in the eye. I looked down. With both hands, she wiped my tear-stained face dry and then grabbed me by the shoulders. "Listen to me, son. I'm really sorry. I'm really sorry I didn't tell you sooner. Believe me; this isn't the sort of thing you just talk about the way I told you about my past. And I'm sorry I've got you mixed up in all this too. I'm sorry I insulted you. Can you forgive me? I'm just a bit on edge, that's all. But I love you as you are. I'm your mother; you can trust me. And now, help me, please. Stop crying. Help me. Please forgive me. I'm sorry. Let's go! OK?"

I didn't look up. I simply nodded. My reply was yes. Mbila sighed. Was she relieved she'd managed to persuade me? Was she pleased she'd crushed me like that? Was it just lip service, just a measly apology? I was angry. I was very angry with my mother. But what good was it? As she said, she was my mother. If she asked me to help her, why wouldn't I? Hadn't I always been her business partner?

My fear transformed into confidence. There was no doubt about it; I was my mother's business partner, her associate. And I wasn't planning on giving up that position. I wanted to remain her loyal friend. Hadn't I lied for her from a tender age, saying she wasn't there when people came looking for their mbongo? Hadn't I looked ever so innocent and lied to those guys who wouldn't take no for an answer and demanded all sorts of things from her? Hadn't I helped her pick out the dress that got her the most clients? Hadn't I been promoted to the position of personal psychologist? Hadn't I called her the luxury brand in the AP? And if I'd done all that, then why wouldn't I transport these little pellets like she asked? After all, a few little pellets down there wasn't all that bad! Looking back, they were even a bit like a sex toy, a sort of anal rosary.

I wiped away my tears, rubbed my nose, and asked, "So what's next?"

"Nothing special, just walk. Walk beside me, like normal. Don't make any sort of movement that could attract attention. Walk beside me, arm in arm, the way we always do. Don't be scared. It'll be fine. Perfectly fine, I'm sure of it."

"OK," I replied. "Let's not waste any more time. Let's go."

I walked beside my mother. We were together, inseparable as usual, arm in arm. The saying "Like mother, like son" had never been truer about my coterie with Mbila. We walked down rue de Berne to rue Sismondi. My mother made sure she greeted a few colleagues on the way. We bumped into Bélen at the junction between rue Sismondi and rue des Pâquis.

"Hey, beautiful Mbila," Belén shouted in the thick Hispanic accent she'd never lost. "Working with our baby tonight, are you?"

"Yes, darling," replied Mbila, smiling, totally relaxed. "Who knows? Maybe Dipita will get me lots-lots of clients tonight."

"Oh yes, I'm sure he will," agreed Bélen before saying goodbye.

I had no idea where my mother was taking me. Each time I asked her where we were going, she just said, "Keep walking and don't ask any questions."

We walked down rue des Pâquis for a bit before turning left toward the place des Alpes.

A few more meters and we arrived at the super chic Richemond Hotel. My mother stopped dead and looked carefully at a few guys in suits and ties, all members of Geneva high society. The Geneva that only ever looks down on people like us, right down, in fact. The men with cigars sipped merrily on champagne that bubbled like a fizzy tablet had been dropped in their glasses.

"Is this it?" I asked.

"No. No, it's not here. I was just looking at those men. Don't they look like good clients for your wolowoss mother?"

"Oh, yes. That's exactly what I was going to say. But come on; we've got other fish to fry before we chase them. Let's go."

"You're right, son. I'm so silly." We laughed like two old cotas.

As we continued on our way to our mystery destination, a police siren suddenly wailed in the distance. We both panicked. We looked at each other. What should we do? The fear I thought I'd tamed reared its head again at breakneck speed; it was even worse now. It hit me so hard I thought I'd faint. The thing I was most afraid of in the world seemed to be knocking at my heart: prison. Prison? Oh no! Not that! Not me. Especially since I had nothing to do with this whatsoever. My mother was the one who had dragged me down this dark, dangerous path. I saw myself splashed not only across the front pages of the papers in French-speaking Switzerland but the rest of the country too. *La Tribune de Genève* would run the scoop for weeks. They'd say we were a family of drug dealers! Mother: wolowoss. Son: well . . . faggot! Common denominator: pill pushers. The thought of it made me want to throw up. The louder the siren got, the stronger the urge became.

I turned to my mother, who was still clinging to my arm.

"I'm going to throw up," I mumbled.

"No, my dear, this really isn't the time."

"The police, the police are coming. The mbéré," I said.

"I know. Nothing to worry about. Just stay calm. They're not coming for us," my mother reassured me.

"How do you know?" I asked.

"I'm used to it. Calm down, for goodness' sake," she murmured.

"I can't."

"Yes, you can. Just concentrate and breathe."

"I don't feel very well," I stammered again.

"I know. Breathe. Take a few deep breaths. You'll be OK."

"Why on earth did you bring me with you?" I asked her.

"We're not getting into that again, OK? Let's be strong. Listen, we need to split up. Maybe you're right. You never know; maybe those mbéré are looking for us. Maybe those guys pulled a swift one on me. I didn't make it easy for them last time they called. You never know. Go on straight ahead, over there, the other side of the road, along the lake, toward the bains des Pâquis. We can meet on quai Wilson. Know it?"

Quai Wilson? Of course I knew it. I knew quai Wilson very well. It was where Saarinen and I used to spend hours chatting and playing every afternoon. Saarinen was like Cousin Loudmouth Pitou. I often called him Loudmouth Saarinen. And just like Pitou, Saarinen always had something to yack-yack about! One of his favorite stories was about Geneva underwater. He said torrential rains would pour down on Geneva for days and weeks on end. The water in the lake would rise to unimaginable levels and reach the quayside. He said a huge wave would be released from the bed of the lake and crash down onto the blocks of luxury apartments along quai Mont Blanc and quai Wilson, the way the prostitutes flood out onto rue de Berne and rue Sismondi. He said all the grand hotels in the area would collapse, along with all the guests in their luxurious rooms who splashed their mbongo on their every whim, forgetting to help poor children like us. Sometimes he'd adopt a serious tone, like a Bantu storyteller. *And quai Wilson shall be swallowed up, destroyed completely by the water from the lake. And there shall be chaos everywhere, all over Geneva! Chaos.* Hundreds of children would lose their lives in the waters of the lake. But businessmen and bankers would be the first to be swept away, punished for not wanting to help the poor. He said I had definitely made the right decision to become a designer and not a banker. There would be a huge human soup, bodies would float on the floodwaters like ducks and swans. Heaps of bodies would rival the boats, owned by the wealthy, that pollute the lake. And picnic lovers would be caught up in the tidal wave too, oh yes! Because they spend all their time fighting for a spot on the artificial beach at the bains des Pâquis. Oh! What a truckload of anger Saarinen had in his belly when it came to those Sunday-morning picnickers who never left any space for us, the poor little children whose mothers worked late into the night, or right through the night, in fact! I was scared stiff the first time he told me that the Witch of the Lake, Genévroina, a beautiful siren with a golden tail and pitch-black hair that sparkled with diamonds, would rise up from the murky waters. She would rise up high, right up to the sky. She would roar with laughter! *Ha ha ha!* Like the bad guys in cartoons. With a terrifying look in his eye, he swore that Genévroina would feed on the corpses floating on the murky waters, drinking the human soup served up to her. She would lick the corners of her huge mouth with her long reptilian tongue to catch any human innards that tried to escape. He told me that lots—lots and lots—of people would die; there would be few survivors. Children would search for their parents without success. Parents would search for their children without ever finding a single trace of them. Their bodies would be swallowed up by the wild, gaping mouth of the Genévroina siren. Raising his hands toward the sky, my friend Saarinen shouted, "It shall be known as the GE-NE-VA FLOOD!"

Absolutely terrified, heart in my mouth, I had run as hard as I could, ignoring all the red lights, back to rue de Berne where I found my mother busy at work. Worried, she asked, "What's wrong, son? Where's your friend Saarinen?"

"Mama, Mama," I replied, out of breath. "Saarinen says . . . says . . . says there'll be a flood in Ge . . . Ge . . . Geneva."

"What?"

"A . . . a . . . flood."

"Huh?"

"He says the water will come up over quai Wil . . . Wil . . . quai Wilson and everyone will die. Mama, I'm scared for you. I'm scared for me too. I'm really scared, even if Saarinen says that the Witch of the Lake, the nasty Genévroina, won't eat us, won't eat the poor. I'm . . . I'm . . . I'm . . . really scared. Do you think we'll die in the Geneva Flood?"

My mother burst out laughing. She phoned Bélen, Saarinen's mother, and the rest of her colleagues to tell them all about something she called kid nonsense. The AP girls laughed and laughed and warned, "If you aren't good for your mothers, there'll be a big flood in Geneva, and you'll be the only one who dies. But if you're a good boy and go back and play with Saarinen on quai Wilson, then there won't be any floods." No way! I was never going back to play with Saarinen, who always gave me the heebie-jeebies with his stories about those floods. I'd rather go around to Blond

Silvia or Brunette Romaine's to pamper their Barbies and brush the dolls' hair. It was much more fun.

Just as I was about to leave my mother and cross quai Mont Blanc to walk along the lake and meet her further down on quai Wilson, the police siren came closer. The patrol car stopped right in front of us.

"Stop! Stop right there," ordered the police officers as they got out.

My mother obeyed without batting an eyelid. I did too. Calmly, but my heart was on overdrive.

"What's the matter?" I asked innocently, sounding surprised.

One of the police officers, a tall, dark-haired guy as cranky as a guard dog, approached us. He ordered us to raise our hands, which we did immediately. While the dark-haired police officer frisked my mother, the other one searched me. I felt remarkably relaxed. Even now, I wonder how I managed to convince myself of my innocence so well that I remained calm in front of those mbéré. They didn't find anything suspicious on us. They ordered us to open our mouths wide, like patients at the doctors. It was ridiculous and, above all, humiliating, but we had to obey. They shone their torches down our throats. Niet. Didn't find a thing. They took my mother's handbag and rifled through it. All her belongings ended up on the ground: lipliners, makeup bag, makeup brush, foundation applicator, condoms, eyeliner, hand cream, face cream, a white envelope marked "invitation" and, most importantly, her red passport with a white cross.

The police officers took a quick look inside the envelope, which seemed to contain an invitation. They didn't dwell on it. They checked my mother's passport and realized they were dealing with a sweet, angelic Swiss woman. They also checked my identity and found my Swiss ID card—another good, dark-skinned angel. Clearly reassured, the police officers put my mother's belongings back into her handbag, one by one, and returned it to her. They apologized and got back into their patrol car. They didn't give any reason for the search whatsoever. Seeing that they'd given up, I took advantage of the situation to object. "What kind of Geneva is this? Is Geneva still a Republic of Human Rights? Isn't this racist? Isn't this blatant racism? How can you even dare to shame poor, innocent citizens in this way? I think I'll have to tell the press about this." My mother played along like a real pro and told me to drop it. She tried to get me to calm down. But oh no. No way was I going to calm down. I shouted even louder. I was angry, furious, in fact, with these police officers who had just let two big drug dealers go.

The patrol car started up and stuttered off. An air of peace blew into our hearts. Free, my mother and I let out huge sighs of relief. My mother praised my efforts. If she could have, she'd have promoted me again. I think she'd have given me a special medal in recognition of my bravery. I was her hero, her superman.

We walked a few more meters along the lake and reached quai Wilson. A majestic hotel towered up over the rest of the buildings.

"This is the drop-off point," said my mother.

At the entrance, a bellboy as tall and skinny as a string of spaghetti bowed so low as he opened the door that he looked like he wanted to polish our shoes. His red uniform drowned his tiny-tiny body. Everything hung loose on him; even his cap slid down over his eyes.

"We have an appointment," my mother whispered to him in an exaggerated Geneva accent. I grimaced because she usually has a thick Bassa accent. But depending on the context, she changes her accent to give the impression she's a born and bred local.

The spaghetti-string bellboy asked us to follow him to the reception desk, like we'd get lost without his help.

As we crossed the small lobby leading to the reception, I took a moment to admire the luxury around us. I'd never seen anything like it before. I'd grown up in Geneva, a city where the social inequalities are often as glaring as they are offensive. My mother and I lived in a hovel on rue de Berne, but only a few meters away, rich fat cats lived in breathtakingly luxurious hotels: the Richemond, the Hotel d'Angleterre, the Kempinski, the President Wilson and all the rest. I'd seen exactly the same thing back in Ngodi-Akwa during my holidays in Cameroon. On one side, you had a large proportion of the population crammed into the most revolting shanty towns you've ever seen with no sort of work whatsoever, and on the other side, just a few meters away, the filthy rich lived in super modern villas. Looking at the luxury in this hotel, I reckoned that Saarinen's flood was bound to happen one day.

"Good evening, madam," my mother said to the blond, heavily made-up receptionist. "We have an appointment with a gentleman here."

"Does he have a reservation?" asked the receptionist.

"Yes, I think so," my mother replied.

"Under which name?"

"Oyono Bivondo."

"Yes, madam. He's over there, on the left, in the lounge bar."

So my mother was still in touch with that crook Oyono Bivondo, that guy who had exploited her for two long years. Disappointed, I thought there was no way Mbila could ever surprise me again. That evening, she'd shown me just how far she could fall-fall. So why should I be surprised she was still hanging around with a guy like that?

Oyono Bivondo was sitting in a corner of the skylight bar. He got up when he saw Mbila. He scowled at her. Mbila made brief introductions. "This is Dipita, my son." It was the first time I'd ever seen my biological father, in person, in the flesh. He reached out his hand and greeted me coldly, as though I was the one who had a problem with him. What did I care? Well, I had at least expected him to behave like Mr. Rappard, to have a few manners like a decent person, to give Mama the chance to suggest we drink a cup of tea, just the three of us . . . but there was zilch. After giving him a quick once-over, I thought he must be like one of those gigolo bastards, or even one of those feymen that Charlotte the hairdresser talked about. I expected him to take a closer look at me, to perhaps search for some sign of resemblance. I thought he might say he had missed me, ask if I wanted some sort of support for my studies, or perhaps even offer help for my comrade Démoney. But there was nothing. He didn't give me a second glance. He didn't have any time to waste. We were already pretty late.

Oyono was dying to get it over with. We needed to deliver the goods he was waiting for, pronto. My mother looked at him, and he immediately pointed toward the bathrooms.

Like two women ready to burst, Mbila and I headed into the ladies' bathrooms. My mother grabbed three cotton towels the hotel provided for its patrons and two small plastic bags. We locked ourselves into a cubicle. And that's when the dubious operation to expel our goods began.

Mbila took the envelope with "invitation" on it out of her bag, the envelope the police officers hadn't bother to look at properly. She produced two tiny tablets and ordered me to open my mouth. "Go on, take that; it'll help you get it all out quickly," she said. And that's precisely what happened. The laxative took immediate effect. Sitting comfortably on the toilet seat, I started by getting rid of the pellets from my rectum without a problem. The five other pellets in my stomach followed, one by one.

Once I'd been emptied, I wiped myself clean and got dressed again. My mother squeezed past me in the narrow cubicle to stop me from making the huge mistake of flushing the toilet. She didn't want to lose any of our precious pellets. She looked down into the toilet bowl for our shit-covered manna. With bare hands, she reached in and carefully picked out each of the pellets, one by one, taking care not to burst them. There was a small sink in the cubicle where she quick-quick rinsed the pellets before drying them with the towels she had taken. "Good work, son. You're better than a pro." I smiled, proud to receive my mother's praise.

Then it was her turn. She purged herself with skill and dexterity. From time to time, she sighed a little and grimaced slightly. Then *plop, plop!* I heard the pellets drop out, one by one. As soon as she had birthed all of the pellets, Mbila started the whole rinsing business again. All in all, we had fifty-five cocaine pellets tidily packed into the plastic bags. Mbila slipped them gently into her handbag. She washed her face, dried it with the towels she hadn't used, applied a little face cream, and redid her makeup. She added a few squirts of perfume. She finished freshening up and looked beautiful, as beautiful as ever. She was worlds apart from the Lucifer I'd seen in her bedroom just a few hours earlier. She was radiant, and you wouldn't have had a clue she had violated me not long before. Mbila turned to me and said, "I don't know how to thank you. You really saved me. I promise you one thing—I'll never ask you to do anything like that again. And I hope you'll never do anything like that again either. Forget everything that happened tonight, and above all, never say a word to anyone. OK?"

"Yes, Mama."

"Not even William."

"Don't worry. It'll stay between us."

"You're an angel, son. I'm counting on you to continue your studies, stay out of trouble, and become elastic."

"No, Mama, it's the elasticity of demand in relation to price."

XIII

I TRY TO STOP thinking about William. But it's impossible. Every day, his smile, his gaze, his face occupy my thoughts. It feels like he's right here with me in my cell, in my bed, beside me, holding me. Sometimes I see him in the prison corridors, the showers, the dining hall.

This morning, I took my notebook out of the drawer in my small bedside table. I saw the Bible they gave me when I entered prison lying there too. As far as I'm concerned, it's just there for decoration. I haven't opened it once. I don't really need to read it or even pray, for that matter, since the prison chaplain says he intercedes fervently on our behalf, asking God to forgive us for the evil that brought us to this prison.

For the past few days, I've been trying to write a few lines about William. And I'm fed up; I've had enough because I don't know where to start. Yet I have to talk about him. Otherwise, I wouldn't be telling the whole story. But whenever I think about him, my concentration flags, fades. I lose direction.

I went down to the carpentry workshop early-early this morning to try and clear my head. But it's always the same down there. The sawing, gluing, and sanding machines never change. They never move, obviously. The supervisor is always there, encouraging the guys. *Doing time in prison isn't the end of the world*, he repeats. This endless-endless monotony only makes me feel restless and bored. Let's not even mention the damned overcrowding. All those lovely people virtually stepping on your toes; all those faces you want to be rid of for even just a day but have to bear; all that noise, prisoners chattering, guards striding slowly but surely down the halls, key chains jangling, the planing machines, the TVs and radios blaring all day.

The racket made me walk right back out of the workshop, my notebook tucked under my arm. I wanted to gather my thoughts in my cell and find the right words to talk about William.

I think I loved William in a way I'd never loved anyone before. I'm sure part of the reason I loved him was because I felt like I'd had a lucky break. Any time I saw myself in a mirror, I wondered how a handsome young man like William could be in love with me. We were like Beauty and the Beast.

I didn't think I looked fresh-fresh at all. The sight of my own face made me feel sick. I had the most repulsive acne everywhere. And millions of blackheads too. The blemishes were all the more obvious and revolting because my skin's quite light. No cream or gel in the world could solve those problems. And then there was my nose—it was oh so flat. Mbila used to tease me about it, saying she could turn it into a vacuum cleaner. My puny physique and spindly legs really gave me a complex. My big almond-shaped eyes were the only thing I was halfway happy about. But were those eyes enough to justify William's ndolo for me?

My love for William wasn't just physical, even though, compared to me, he looked like he came from another planet. He had other subtler charms that made me feel even more blessed. William had a certain way about him, and I wasn't the only one singing his praises. What my mother liked most, for example, was his humble side. He was respectful, almost servile. Any time he came around, he'd help out. He didn't hesitate to vacuum the entire flat, clean the bathroom, or even iron my mother's frilly dresses. Since I hated doing the washing up and my mother was forever afraid of ruining her manicure, our sink was often piled high with disgustingly dirty dishes. Disappointed that I was so lazy, my mother knew she could count on William's subservience. Without moaning, he'd slip on the pink gloves and get to work. *Look, Dipita, there's a child who has been brought up well,* my mother would say.

There was also something instinctively naive about William. You could see it in his eyes, in his smile, in his gentle manners. Maybe that's why I wanted to hold his hand whenever we walked down the street. I didn't hold it to show how I felt about him. No, I was almost like a father who was afraid his son would be run over by a car at the next junction. And I loved that power, that responsibility—it was the only thing I had to help balance our relationship a bit.

I tried to please William by doing things he liked. And what he liked most—apart from *those* things—was listening to tales from Africa. I told him stories as though they had really happened.

One evening, as my mother showed an endless string of clients in and out of her room, William and I were alone in my room. I rested my head on his chest, he played with my hair, and all sorts of stories came to me, things I simply made up. That night, I told him about Nigerians who could breathe fire from the bottom of their bellies like dragons. I told him that during the Biafran War in the late 1960s, the Nigerian Igbo people spat huge flames out of their stomachs to terrorize and intimidate their Hausa and Yoruba enemies, who accused them of stealing oil. But, above all, the Hausa and Yoruba people believed that the Igbo people had hidden barrels of oil in their big bellies. That's why they could breathe fire! That's what I told William, and he was amazed.

I also told him about Maagne, a Bamiliké mother from the west of Cameroon who gave birth to a strange baby. Maagne was a young woman who was forever under pressure from her in-laws because she had failed to bring at least one son into the world, an heir. After giving birth to six girls, this young Bamiliké mother decided to ask a halan mimbou for help. The charlatan gave her a potion containing toad saliva as the main ingredient. Full of hope, she swallowed the potion. A few weeks later, she fell pregnant. The young woman finally gave birth to a boy—but the child had a toad's head. Oh yes, a human with warts all over his body, bulging eyes, and a round-round mouth. As soon as the baby opened its mouth, it croak-croaked like a real toad.

～

I've gone back and read everything I managed to write about William. Not bad, not bad at all. It'll do. But I think I need to write a bit more. I want to talk about our brotherly bond, for example. Yes, William's my brother because we're both called Rappard.

I'm talking nonsense. William isn't my brother. We don't share any blood ties, never mind the same womb, because William's got his mother and I've got Mbila. His mother is called Papusha. I've met her a few times. She's an extremely beautiful blond Russian. She's got long legs and acts like she was brought up well. When I first saw her, I could immediately see where William's good looks and sensitive soul came from. Papusha's a wolowoss too; well, she's an escort girl, as William always liked to correct me. Since I couldn't see any difference between a wolowoss and an escort girl, William had to explain that escort girls didn't work on the street but in big hotels. She was treated with more respect and, above all, paid more.

I'd never been brave enough to tell William I found it infuriating—insulting, even—that he insisted on judging our mothers' professions differently. Deep down, I'm still a bit bitter about it, to be honest. It felt like William had everything and I had nothing: he was handsome, and I was anything but; he was white, and I was dark-dark; he had a mother who frequented the city's big hotels as an escort girl, while mine made do with her patch on the street as a hooker in rue de Berne. This simmering unconfessed hate had been stifled by my feelings for William and the joy I felt at being his boyfriend. I'd also found comfort in my friend Saarinen's apocalyptic tale. I took comfort in the thought that, unlike Papusha, my mother wouldn't be gobbled up by the siren Genévroina when the Geneva Flood arrived.

XIV

TIME SEEMS to be dragging at a snail's pace this afternoon. I've had enough of sitting in my cell reflecting on my short life. Maybe a bit of exercise or manual labor will help me relax. So I head down to the carpentry workshop and join in.

There are about twenty prisoners in the workshop. We're divided into groups of three or four to work on joint projects. A few guys want to make a coffee table. "It's the easiest thing to make," says our supervisor, "but you need to pay attention to detail."

Across the room, a group of four inmates from the Balkans are working on a chest of drawers. "That's a pretty ambitious project," reckons the supervisor, proud of their sense of initiative. He smiles at them admiringly, the way you would when your little kid shows you they can read or do mental arithmetic. But it doesn't really surprise me. Berisha, the drop-dead gorgeous Albanian I've talked to a lot, told me he was a carpenter before he ended up here.

My group, on the other hand, doesn't really know what it wants to make. A table? That sounds too easy, even though it would actually require focus and attention to detail. A chest of drawers? That'd be far too difficult. We'd rather leave that to pros like Berisha. Since we don't have a clue what we're doing, we just sand, sand, cut, cut, measure, and remeasure bits of wood. We line them up without really knowing what to do with them. Our supervisor's ideas never really appeal to us, anyway. He suggested making a door or a window frame. Big Okocha, a Nigerian with an ebony complexion and lips as red as a kola nut, replied loudly in his best French, "Une window, sir, nous pas faire that. I mean me, moi, I don do that! Nous in prison ici here. So we don't make a window. Don't make no door no window. Nothing. That's for people who are free." His fellow inmates burst out laughing, and it was a while before they stopped. They were making fun of him, but he thought it was an ovation for being so brave and direct.

I never really pay attention to that sort of thing; it happens so often, especially when Okocha's involved. He yack-yacks all the time about any old thing. Even when he's not speaking, his mere presence makes a noise. When I went to prison, I thought I'd left those one-eyed loudmouths Pitou and Saarinen behind, but here I am with yet another one. I even call him Lo-Oko-Loudmouth. Couldn't he just pull some drawers over his mouth for once? I often feel like telling him to just shut up, to zip it, but I never dare because I'm not exactly in a position to correct anyone, especially not here in prison. I also stay quiet because I want to keep my head down. I still hope they'll pardon me for good behavior. It would let me help my uncle quick-quick.

This manic laughter and banter are constant in my new incarcerated life. Inmates laugh at the slightest thing. They even laugh when it's pretty serious: when one of them sets fire to his mattress and cell, when another is savagely bludgeoned by the guards who say he was disobedient, when someone else languishes in the grip of a merciless flu. They laugh like everything's fine, like prison's just a bit of fun, like it's a playground or day care for us dangerous children. They laugh because it might offer a glimmer of hope.

Just a few months ago, I had no idea I'd end up here, laughing in prison. To think that I miraculously escaped a police search with a truckload of cocaine in my belly. Never ever would I have pictured myself here now.

And I'd found true love! William and I were on cloud nine at that point and had been together for just over a year. We were inseparable, conjoined, entangled, one and the same.

⌁

It was summertime in Geneva, and the funfairs were in full swing. The city glowed like burning embers on both sides of the lake. The water sparkled as it reflected the bright lights and colors. Grand carousels and chair swings spun, delighting their passengers. Fun and laughter all around.

William and I struggled our way along the stunning yet packed quai Mont Blanc. People were walking in all directions on the quayside that had been closed to traffic. The national holiday had been a few days earlier, and Geneva was about to put on a special fireworks display. It was August 4, and in addition to all the other festivities, it was my mother's birthday.

A few hours later, just before 10:00 p.m., all the lights were switched off. Geneva was plunged into darkness. William and I had managed to find a spot near the lakeside promenade. We were holding hands, surrounded by the crowd impatiently waiting for the fireworks. William's warm hand communicated his deepest feelings for me—ndolo, of course. Nothing but love. My spine tingled.

When the fireworks were over, William yawned as a way of telling me how tired he was. I could see it in his eyes. So I suggested he spend the night with me. It was my mother's birthday. She was bound to be having a good time with her AP friends—we'd have the apartment to ourselves.

"No, not tonight. I'm going to head home and sleep at my mum's place in Bernex. I need a bit of time to myself right now."

"Is everything OK?"

"Yes, everything's fine. Don't worry. I'm just a bit tired and need some rest."

A flash of jealousy ran through me, and I glared at him. I couldn't understand why William was leaving me like that after we'd had such a nice time together. I still wanted him. My need to be with him was not yet satiated—it never was, in fact. I wanted more, ever more.

William must have seen I was worried from the expression on my face. He tried to comfort me. He hugged me, whispering softly, "I love you, little foal." I felt somewhat reassured, but it didn't quench the flame of jealousy within me entirely.

We went our separate ways. I headed back to 39 rue de Berne. The only thing I was thinking about was going home, lying on my bed, and hugging my feather pillow as I thought of William.

I touched myself for a long time that night. As my fingers played with my nipples, I imagined William doing the same with his teeth. Legs spread, I gently slid a finger inside me. Compared to what William gave me, it was only symbolic.

William was *there*, his body, his scent, his breath, his image, in my head, in my imagination, in my room, on me, in me, deep inside of me. There, his agile hips moving back and forth in time. He was there, pulling me toward him with his strong, veiny arms. Our bodies fused. This imagined fusion made my eyes roll back. William continued caressing me, rubbing me. To and fro. He couldn't stop because I was begging him to go on, more and more, harder, faster, and then eventually: ecstasy. A volcanic eruption. All that energy shot out, soiling my body, my face.

After that imagined pleasure, I felt weak, so weak I fell into a deep sleep, hugging my William-pillow tight. I slept like a baby for a few minutes. Then I was woken by the horns beeping in the street and felt a huge hole in my belly. I was hungry.

All I'd eaten that day had been a few churros with cinnamon sugar at the funfair a few hours earlier. I decided to get a grilled-grilled chicken kebab from one of the kebab shops nearby.

I headed to Ali Kebab.

Ali must have been from the Balkans. I didn't know which country, exactly. He was a tall, dark-haired guy with swarthy skin and a lot of hair. A simple man who was always smiling.

He greeted me in his best French. But what did I care about his French? I just liked him because he always added a little extra grilled-grilled chicken to my kebab.

"So, my friend, we make chicken kebab like usual?" he asked me.

"Yes, Ali! My usual chicken kebab. And no spicy sauce, please."

"No! Not spicy! Me no spicy sauce in kebab you. Chicken kebab like uuuusual."

"Great! Ali, you know what I like. Hey, where's the bathroom?" I asked.

"What? Don't understand."

"Bath-room," I repeated. "Bath-room, pee-pee, poo-poo," I repeated.

"Oh yes! There!" he said, pointing.

I headed toward the bathroom in Ali's kebab shop, dying to go. I pushed the door, and it opened easily; it wasn't locked.

And that's when I saw it! It was outrageous! William doing naughty things with my best friend, Saarinen. The flood!

XV

OVER THE NEXT few days, I completely lost my appetite. Mbila did her best to get me to eat and, above all, tell her what was bothering me. But niet, I didn't belch a word. For days, I remained mute, silent, lost, dazed, confused. I was holed up not just in my room but in a cache of happy memories where William was the cherished treasure and other delightful images danced around him. Like our unexpected encounter outside the Meat Market, our first hot-hot night together, our mothers' blessing, the end of my dalliances with suicide, our passionate relationship that had lasted just over a year . . . all those wonderful memories had run aground on this flagrant betrayal.

What do you do when you know you've been betrayed? What do you say when you make as shocking a discovery as I just had? William! Oh, William! For how long had he been getting Saarinen to eat his plantain? Why? Why had he done that to me? The question kept turning in my head. It made me dizzy. Why had he done that to me? Why had he done that to me, Dipita? Hadn't he just told me he loved me a few hours earlier? That's what he'd said, and it was true. It was true; I was sure of it. I'd seen it in his eyes. It was true because William couldn't just betray me like that, no. He couldn't cheat on me. He wasn't a world champion in deceit. He wasn't even an amateur. I swear he loved me! I'd felt all that ndolo through his silky soft skin as he held me tight. I'd felt it in his gentle, deep voice, in the pleasant scent of his forever moist underarms, in the firmness of his ever so appetizing plantain, in our heady nocturnal rendezvous, in the tender words he wrapped around me.

I remember him resting his head on my shoulder and whispering in my ear: *You're all I need to be happy*. He had murmured other sweet nothings—not an endless stream; William didn't just spout out words. Sometimes, when he really went for it, he'd say I was the Cenovis on his morning toast, the salt in his Le Parfait jar, the milk in his renversé, the ice cubes in his Suze, the kirsch in his fondue.

And one thing I can't leave out is how he'd say, "You're my type." Those few words—"you're my type"—well, they were so clear and meant so much to me. They gave me some of the confidence I so desperately needed. My chest puffed with pride. Those words meant someone could like me, that I could tick the right boxes. It sounded so nice each time he whispered that phrase in my ear that I felt like I was on cloud nine, dancing the Bi-ZiZi, eating grilled grasshoppers. I felt good, even though sometimes I wondered, Am I really his type? Me? But what type of guy am I? The image I had of myself was just a spotty little Black wimp who looked a lot like a cockroach.

You'll say beauty's on the inside. OK, well, let's say beauty's on the inside, but what sort of beauty was there inside me, deep down? I was jealous, unkind, introverted, a scaredy-cat, mougou—you know. That's it, the very definition of mougou. I was fearful, even though my mother kept saying I was a hero, especially after that business with the drugs. Well, maybe I was Mbila's hero. But be that as it may, did it really mean I had what it took to be William's type? Yet despite my enormous Bantu nose, as wide as the Matterhorn, despite my skinny frame, despite the color of my skin, despite my lack of inner beauty, yes, despite all that, I was still William's type!

And if I really was his type, then why had he done that to me? Why had he loved me so much he'd cheated on me? And who had he cheated on me with? That was a jab too far! He could have done it with someone else, a guy I didn't know, but not with him, not with Saarinen, for me to discover which way he leaned at the same time. Saarinen was *like that* too, then, like the white men Uncle Démoney talked about!

Saarinen and William together, screwing it all up? No, I didn't want to admit it, even though I'd seen them in action. And where had they been? There, at it, in the bathroom in nice Ali's kebab shop. It hurt too much.

The situation was so critical that Mbila convened an urgent AP meeting. Due to its extraordinary nature, the meeting didn't take place in our living room but in my bedroom. There I was, wasting away, lying in my bed. The bed where I could still smell and feel William's presence.

The AP girls were worried about my health, my corpse-like body, my sudden worrying weight loss. I was as skinny as Uncle Démoney's early retirement pension.

"I'm sure it's because of William," began Charlotte, an expert in all that cutesy Chéri Coco couple stuff.

"I think you're right," agreed Belén, unaware that her son, Saarinen, was also part of the fuck-up making me sick.

"I tried calling him a few times," added Mama, "but I keep getting his voice mail. I don't know what's going on."

"Oh, kids today!" shouted Charlotte. "Their romances are so hard to understand."

"Girls," said Maïmouna, "let's not overthink this. We've managed to hold our own as hookers in our classy Pâquis neighborhood, so we're not going to let a little William like-like that give us grief by getting our son into this state. Let's go to his place right now and give him a good thrashing!"

The room echoed with endless *You're so right, Maïmouna! That's the honest truth, Maï!* One by one, the AP girls voiced their support for the suggested punishment. The ruling appeared to have been handed down. They'd soon give William what he deserved. Yeah! A wave of satisfaction flooded my heart and soul. If pain and hate hadn't paralyzed the muscles in my face, I'm sure I'd have smiled at the thought of them giving him a good thrashing. I'd even have given them a standing ovation. Revenge can feel so good! Oh, how I wanted them to beat him up, that bastard: tie him up, shock him with a few kilowatts of nuclear electricity, burn his *thing* with some melted candle wax, or better still, a lit cigarette. I even wanted them to violate him, yes, with a baseball bat after they'd broken one of his ribs. I wanted all of that, wanted to see him hurt in all those ways. Eye-for-an-eye revenge had settled in my belly, and I was bloated with rage.

"No, ladies," said Mbila, trying to dampen their enthusiasm. "We're not in Ngodi-Akwa now, are we? We're in a country with laws. And you don't do that sort of thing in a country that applies the rule of law."

A loud, disapproving *ah* rippled through the room. I closed my eyes to shut out the rest of the meeting. My mind fled elsewhere, nowhere, into the void deep within me, down into the twists and turns of my disappointment. The girls grumbled for a few minutes after my mother's objection. It was a hot-hot debate. They couldn't agree on what to do about William. Charlotte took the floor again, like a good president.

"Girls! Girls! Mbila's right. We're in Geneva after all. And we can't just do whatever we want in Geneva, even if we live in the Pâquis . . . We need to keep our cool. Calmos! Calmos, ladies! Instead of getting mixed up in a romance that's gone tchakla, fallen apart, eh, and heading out to beat up the young man in his mother's home, we'd be better off helping our son Dipita. Do I have to remind you he hasn't eaten a thing for four days?"

"Oh, darling, you must eat," Maïmouna said all of a sudden, kneeling beside my bed. "You know, there's food here, so you might as well enjoy it. Back in Africa, lots of children in Rwanda don't have any food."

"I even made the accra banana he loves, his auntie Bilolo's. Not even that could tempt him. He wouldn't even take a tiny bite. Nothing. Nothing at all. He won't touch a thing."

Amid my mothers' tempestuous discussions, my heart continued to swell with bitterness. Despite their care and concern, I couldn't get rid of that image of William on top of Saarinen. I kept seeing my guy—shorts down, ass bare, hands gripping Saarinen's white skin. The image haunted me. I wanted to force down even a tiny bite of accra banana, just to keep Maïmouna happy. I could have done it just to reassure Mbila, who'd never looked so worried in her life. Yes, I could have tried to swallow something, but fury had killed off any hint of appetite whatsoever, and I brushed aside my mothers' pleas. The hatred within me grew, swiftly spreading like a merciless virus. There was despair too, deep despair—how would I ever meet anyone like William again? Deep down, I'd always felt I didn't deserve his love. I'd never felt that the relationship was balanced, even though of course William kept telling me I was his type. I'd always had the feeling I was in a relationship I didn't deserve. William was too good, too handsome, much too good and handsome for me.

Total despair . . . How could I forget a man like William when I knew I had no chance of finding even a tiny scrap of love like that again? Who would want me? Not even the last pig alive! The gay scene is vicious, merciless. No one at the Meat Market likes fat guys, skinny guys, or Asians, never mind Blacks. Who would ever have me, a poor Black guy with no hidden charms? My uncle was right after all—being *like that* really is only for white guys. For us Black guys, it's even harder to prove otherwise.

The following evening, I managed to drag myself out of my room while my mother was at work (may the Lord bless her noble work!). I'd locked myself away for four days as I tried to digest my misfortune. My hunger strike had weakened me. I shivered. There's no denying I was already pretty puny, but by then I was positively Ethiopian. I don't need to tell you that it only made my chronic lack of self-esteem worse. I felt like a complete loser, so lame, a total failure times ten. I looked at my belly, my arms, my hands, and I could only come to one conclusion: I was ugly. Nothing else. Ugly. I wasn't anyone's type!

Weighed down by these doubts and worries, my head drooped. I grabbed at furniture to steady myself as I slowly made my way to the kitchen. A plate of accra banana was waiting for me. I took one and bit into it slowly. All my holidays in Cameroon as a child gradually came back. For a few seconds, the memories blotted out the image of betrayal that tormented me. I saw Auntie Bilolo again, smiling as she peeled her cooking bananas and kneaded the dough for her accra banana. I saw her wandering around the Ngodi-Akwa market lanes, her platter perched on her head. I wanted to ask her for help because I knew she possessed a mother's love that could soothe any pain.

I managed to eat three accra banana from the mountain my mother had fried. They didn't taste quite like the ones Auntie made back in Cameroon. No surprise, of course, since my mother had made them with bananas imported from goodness knows where and not with the cooking bananas we have back home, the green ones the monkeys like.

The accra banana tumbled into my empty belly. I felt a slight pang that made me bite my lip. Thankfully, the pain soon trotted off. I made myself a cup of black tea to help digest the accra banana. As I made it, I remembered that first evening when I'd struggled to make those two little cups of tea for William and me—the evening he came into the kitchen and asked *Hey, Dipita, are you gay?* I remembered the cups I had dropped, the shards on the kitchen floor. I remembered the first time I kissed William and everything else. I remembered it all and couldn't stop myself from crying as I halfheartedly stirred my tea. My tears splashed into my cup.

Unanswered questions stabbed my head like a crown of thorns. Where was he now? What was he doing? Was he in someone else's arms? Was he in my friend Saarinen's arms? Did he know I was suffering? Did he share my pain? Was he going to break up with me or try to win me back? How could I ever live without him? Did he feel any sort of regret for the pain he had caused me? And why should he?

I turned absentmindedly toward the window of our bright kitchen, as though it might offer an answer to all my questions. But far from reassuring me, the window threw me into a panic. I was presented with my reflection. I saw myself naked, stark naked, thinner than usual. I was almost skeletal, and my ribs and collar bones jutted out. I slowly walked toward my reflection. Hands trembling, I brushed it, stroked it, touched it. This reflection confirmed how much work I needed to do on my body. I'm sure *that's* why he left me, I heard myself murmur. I fell to my knees, in tears.

Through my tears, I saw a knife beside me. I looked at this weapon for a long time, wondering if I'd have the courage to use it. I grabbed it by the handle. I examined the blade. I wanted to use it. But how? Could it slit the throat of my hate? Could it slice through my jealousy?

Fat beads of sweat dotted my feverish brow. I thought about ending this unbearable suffering. Leaving. Yes, leaving it all. Leaving to be free. Leaving so I'd never see William again.

Leaving to hurt him. Leaving to give him the punishment the AP girls hadn't been able to give him in the end. Leaving . . . How could I accept he'd grown cold toward me? How could I imagine him with someone else? Worse still, how could I admit he had left me for my best friend, Saarinen?

I hesitated. I remembered my mother. My mother? But I'd never had a mother, had I? The images of Mbila violating me with cocaine pellets, forcing me to be a drug trafficker, flashed back. My mother wasn't perfect by any means, but was that enough to put her through this kind of pain? And it wasn't just Mbila. What about Charlotte? And Bélen? And Maïmouna? And the others? And my dear uncle and comrade Démoney? I thought about him and how I wanted to support him financially. I was sure that that sort of help would let him accept me as I was, *like that*. I felt ashamed of wanting to corrupt my comrade's principles. If only I had followed his instructions, if only I hadn't let myself get carried away with those white man's things, I wouldn't be suffering like this now.

I heard a knock at the door. I wanted to respond, but I couldn't get a single word out. All the words and cries rising up from my belly made my uvula quiver, but they faded before I could open my mouth. I was paralyzed by fear.

The knocking at the door continued, but I was unable to show any sign of life. All of a sudden, I heard a voice shout, "Is anyone there?" I froze. It was him. No doubt about it. It was definitely his voice. I'd recognize it anywhere, even in a bustling, deafening crowd. It was William. It was his gravelly voice, not as cheerful as usual, a bit down, yes, timid, as quiet as a child who knows they've done something silly. I heard it again: "Is there anyone there?"

What the heck was he doing here? Why had he come to my place? What did he want to tell me? Oh yeah, I knew. I got it. He was going to spout the usual, yack-yack like any guilty party would in this sort of situation. He'd say he still loved me, right?

Just words, words, words! Like that old Italian song, *Parole! Parole! Parole!* He'd say he missed me, right? *Parole! Parole! Parole!* He'd say he hadn't been able to sleep since the last time we'd seen each other, right? *Parole! Parole! Parole!* He'd say he now realized I was his one true love, right? *Parole! Parole! Parole!* More words he would just cast into the wind . . . But somehow, I still had a shred of pride. Just a shred? Oh no! A strong sense of pride! He was back, finally! He was tiptoeing back to me like the prodigal son. Come here! Come here, my love! Oh, how I missed you. He was coming back to ask me to forgive him . . . A guy like William was coming back to beg me to get back together with him. He was coming to beg me! Who? Me? So I really was his type?

No. I still couldn't get rid of that image of him cheating on me; it was still there, right in front of my eyes.

"Is anyone there?" the voice I knew so well asked again. The front door opened, barely making a sound, and closed again. I heard footsteps disappear into the living room. Then they came toward the kitchen, toward me. My heart was pounding. Overcome by fear, I crouched down. I curled up into a ball. I felt that hou nson. I was ashamed William would find me in such a state of despair.

"Dipita? Are you there?" the voice coming toward the kitchen kept asking. I gulped.

William finally reached the kitchen. "Dipita!" shouted the voice, stunned. I looked up and saw him through what felt like a fog. I think he was wearing hazelnut-brown Bermudas and a vest that showed off his chest. I couldn't stop myself from lingering on his broad shoulders, so attractive, that no longer belonged to me. I got rid of the knife in my hand to banish any suspicions that a suicide could have been committed.

"What are you doing here? Go off and find Saarinen. I'm sure he's waiting for you. You prefer to fuck white butts, right? So go on! He'll give you what I can't. Go to him! Bastard!" I screamed at him.

"What on earth do you mean? Have you gone mad?" William asked.

"He's your type, right? Go after him, like usual. What're you waiting for? You can just go on as you've done from the start. Right?" I yelled.

"Calm down."

"Calm down?"

William didn't respond.

"And where were you? The kebab shop shitters! I thought you'd been brought up better than that, escort mother this, escort mother that, not a street hooker."

"My mother's got nothing to do with it, Dipita!" replied William.

"Come on; your fucking white mother is a wolowoss too! A street hooker! All our mothers are just hookers. Nothing more, nothing less! That's it!" I yelled.

William looked at sea, powerless. I'd done it. Exactly what I wanted—lashed out, given him an uppercut, knocked him out.

He hung his head, stared at his shoes. He looked disarmingly innocent. I cracked my knuckles. A heavy silence settled between us. Only rue de Berne continued to buzz outside. William looked paralyzed. It was my fault he was in this state now. I started to cry. I sniffled. What if I'd been too harsh? What if my anger had pushed him too far? He had come looking for me, after all, come to my place. He'd come to ask me to forgive him. Why shouldn't I give him a second chance? Maybe it was just a little slip, after all. Maybe that sneaky bastard Saarinen had led him into temptation. Yes, that was it; it had been him! He'd wanted to steal my guy. No, I knew my friend Saarinen. He'd never do that . . . It didn't matter which prick had brought this bad luck! Disaster had already struck. The plantain had already been peeled!

I was still looking at my Willy's shoulders. He's all mine! His shoulders are mine. His legs are mine. His body is mine. And that *thing* is mine too! He belongs to me.

If only he'd stop staring at his shoes! I wanted him to look at me. I wanted him to come to me. I wanted him to hold me. I wanted him to whisper some sort of sweet nothing. Anything. Just something, you know! I wanted him to whisper in my ear again that I was his type. I wanted him to tell me I was the one he liked to fuck—only me, no one else, and definitely not Saarinen. I wanted him to swear that he didn't like white ass at all. I wanted us to forget everything. Start from scratch. For it to be like the first time. For him to take me by the hand, lead me to my room, throw me on my bed, pull down my boxers, lick me, slide into me down there, again and again and again . . . I wanted all of it. Was I going to give up a guy like him, like William, just because he'd had a little fling? I wasn't so sure. What? A little fling? He'd cheated on me, after all. It wasn't as easy as that!

My sweet William finally lifted his head and looked at me. I felt happy. The hunger I hadn't felt for four days pricked up. I was still crying. He caught my eye and I looked at the floor. What on earth are you doing, Dipita? Just look at him! Enjoy it! Gobble him up!

He suddenly looked so sorry. He took a step toward me, wanting to hug me, no doubt. Sniffing loudly, I told him to stay away from me. But he took another step, and another. I felt my heart give in. Yes, come on! Come here, my ndolo. Please don't stop; I'm begging you. Don't be a mougou. Come closer. Come here.

William wrapped his arms around me. I melted.

What was happening to me? How could I have let him embrace me? My mothers would have been outraged if they'd seen us. Especially Charlotte. She always said you have to make sure men don't walk all over you. If you stand up to them, you remind them they can also think with their brains, not just their bellies and crotches. But how could I turn down a handsome young man like that? Was he being sincere? I didn't know. All I knew was that he was looking at me the same way he used to when we were alone in my room, when he talked about my designs decorating the walls.

Despite his embrace, I was still torpedoed by a thousand questions. How could I ever trust him again? How could I forget his betrayal? And what if he was still cheating? What if he was still seeing Saarinen or someone else? Anyway, he hadn't even tried to offer any sort of excuse for his infidelity. How long had he been grabbing Saarinen's ass? How long had he been penetrating it? And was Saarinen the only one, or were there other rivals? Wasn't he coming back because we weren't equals? I thought about the relationship between Mbila and Oyono, my progenitor. I got angry as I remembered my mother's past. I didn't want to become like her. I didn't want to feel dependent on a man. Irritated, frustrated, confused by desire, repulsion, and above all, a need for revenge, I broke free of William's embrace. I slapped him. He didn't respond. I slapped him again, harder. No response. Screaming like a madman, I threw myself at him and began to beat him black and blue. I lashed out at him as hard as I could, punching him, kneeing him. Still no response. What a bastard! He didn't want to fight back, didn't want to hit me, didn't try to defend himself, nothing, didn't even try to protect himself. He preferred to just take it. Furious, I shoved him with all my might. He stumbled and fell, hitting his head on the kitchen counter. A trickle of blood ran down his face.

I fell on my knees and leaned over my Willy, who lay motionless on the floor. I held his head. I felt the strange consistency of his blood seep onto my hands. I cried out in despair; I wailed. "William! William!" I shouted, stroking his hair. But he didn't respond. "Willy! Dear Willy!" I repeated, hoping he was only pretending not to hear me. Not a word. His eyes rolled back, and his head fell.

XVI

I'M SITTING in a corner in the carpentry workshop in Champ-Dollon Prison, where I started serving time a few months ago. I was sentenced to five years in prison for William's murder.

I'm only eighteen, so I'll be out by the time I'm twenty-three. But what'll I do once I'm free? Carpentry? Where would I find the physical strength a carpenter needs to wield his hammer and saw? Could I still become a designer? Who would ever wear designs by a murderer who was in the headlines for days? Not even AP hookers would want them!

What will I do with my freedom? How will I help Uncle Démoney? And what about him? How will he manage to wait five years for my help? Does he know what happened? Did Mbila spill the beans? Does he know I've been convicted of murder? The murder of a man I loved to death? And if he does know, what does he think?

I look over at the guys from the Balkans who are gradually making progress with their chest of drawers. I watch them to forget the questions spinning in my head.

How can I clear my head? I study Omar, a young Algerian at the far end of the workshop. At least he'll distract me. He's working on his project alone. No one wants or is able to work with him because he has decided to make a cross, a made-to-measure cross. "A cross? But why?" the supervisor had asked, somewhat surprised.

"I want to die. I want to crucify myself. I want to die crucified like Jesus Christ," the inmate replied, unperturbed and determined.

The entire workshop had burst out laughing. Mainly because Omar is a Muslim. "You get everything in this prison, even guys who want to be crucified," joked one prisoner who had bulked up to a muscly one hundred kilos, far too much for his short height.

I watch Algerian Omar, half entertained, half sneering. I watch him mark out the wood, file it, and sand it down ever so fastidiously. He's almost finished. Maybe it won't be long before he asks the prison authorities for a crucifixion permit. Hopefully they'll give him one, I think, still staring at him; otherwise this won't end well. After all, if he's so sure he wants to die, why not give him the opportunity to do so? Personally, I want to live, more than ever before.

⁓

I've had a few visits from the AP wolowoss since I've been here. They've all come, apart from Mbila, whom I haven't seen since the trial. Belén, Saarinen's mother, seemed sorry to hear that her son was involved in the whole sordid affair. She told me Mbila had been so upset by what I'd done and by my conviction that she'd tried to take her own life. She didn't get into any of the details.

The pain of this prison sentence is eating away at all of us, my mothers and me. Never had my mothers thought the violence and crime they faced in their line of work every day would make its way into their own lives, into their bellies, into their son. Never ever had they imagined that I, their little Dipita whom they loved so much, would be found guilty of such an act.

Charlotte had cried for a long time before asking, "What happened to you? How could you do that to us, son?"

I'm still asking myself the same thing. I can't explain it. Maybe it was a fit of jealousy? Uncontrollable anger? Desire for revenge? Lost bearings? For nights on end, I've racked my brain for even a hint of an answer to the question everyone's asking. Everyone in the Pâquis is wondering how I, Dipita, could have done that, said Belén. Everyone is wondering, even the dealers, she had added.

～

When I see the guard enter the workshop, I think I might have a visitor. Maybe my mother has finally come to see me. The guard whispers in the supervisor's ear who then shouts, "Berisha, you've got a visitor." The good-looking guy from the Balkans sets down his saw, takes off his work gloves, wipes his brow with the back of his right hand, and falls into step with the guard.

I abandon Omar and his calvary cross to linger on Berisha's unique beauty. That guy is so handsome. Just over one meter ninety and eighty kilos. His good-looking head sports a lovely mane of blond hair, which has been cropped short. He's got a slim face with prominent features. His eyes are diamond blue. His shoulders are broad and rippling with muscles. It's not Berisha's good looks per se that fascinate me; it's more his striking resemblance to William. When I look at Berisha, the bitter disappointment that landed me in prison fades a little. I feel like I've been absolved of all guilt. It feels like my slate has been wiped clean because my victim is still alive. When I look at Berisha, I see William again—the same physique, the same mannerisms, the same nonchalance, the same posture, the same smile, the same gaze. Only Berisha's slightly bent nose is different from William's perfectly straight one. Berisha's presence brings out my denial of that dark episode in my life. And despite everything, this denial lets me reconnect, little by little, with a desire to live and break free from fate.

Berisha reminds me of William so much that I feel a certain fondness for him; it comes naturally. I love him like I loved William, but secretly, of course. This somewhat clandestine love reminds me a lot of my long relationship with YoungNCute at the Meat Market.

Every night in the dining hall, or before I'm locked back up in my cell alone, I watch Berisha. I examine every little detail of his face, his appearance, the way he walks. I make sure I'm discreet, though, no need to display my *thing* too much; there's nothing less fun than being *like that* in prison, I think. Alone in my tiny cell, Number 408, I picture Berisha stark naked in his own cell, Number 406, just to the left of mine on the even-numbered side. I see him. I see William. And I close my eyes and touch myself for a long time.

But I can't start touching myself in front of the other prisoners in the workshop this morning. If I did, I'd speed up Omar the Muslim's crucifixion. And I don't want that. So I try to look happy. I force myself to forget Berisha-William, to concentrate on a million and one other things. As my mind wanders, the supervisor's voice suddenly rings out across the room, and I jump. "Dipita, you've got a visitor!"

XVII

IT'S MBILA. Finally! I've been dying for this reunion as much as I've been dreading it. I've missed her.

Even though I look calm on the outside, I'm overjoyed to see Mbila, sitting there in the corner of the visitors' room. I'm happy because even if she isn't the perfect mother, she's been a good business partner, a good associate, a good patient, even.

Mbila has picked a corner away from everyone else. I see her as soon as I enter the room. She looks downcast, like a woman who has lost everything. She looks thinner than usual. I walk toward her, taking small-small steps like I'm not sure I want to see her again. I stop for a moment to take the temperature of the atmosphere in the room. There isn't a hint of joy: everything is gloomy, everything from the dark color of the walls to the sullen expressions of the visitors and prisoners.

There aren't many people in the room, a dozen at most. I see Berisha at a table across the room. He's talking to a young woman who's crying. I think he's trying to comfort her. I wonder whether she's his girlfriend or fiancée because he told me he wasn't married. To quell my sudden, inexplicable pang of jealousy, I tell myself that the young woman is only his sister.

I finally sit down opposite Mama. It feels like she's taken a weight from me. I don't know what exactly, but seeing her here, I suddenly feel freed of a burden that has weighed me down for weeks. It must be the weight of isolation, solitude, imprisonment.

There is a deadly silence between Mbila and me. Neither of us wants to speak first. Why speak? To say what? Is an apology required? And if so, who needs to apologize, and why? Maybe I need to ask her to forgive me for what I did. But where can I find the strength to do that? Just like that? How do you learn to become your mother's son?

There are so many pearls in Mbila's eyes—pearls of affection, compassion, tenderness, pity, but above all, disappointment. Of all those pearls, I choose affection and tenderness. I choose them because I can hear Mbila's eyes say what she can't find the words to express. *Why? Why did you do that to me? Why did you leave me on my own? Why didn't you think about me before you blew a fuse?* And since I don't answer the questions her eyes are so obviously asking, Mbila begins to cry. Her face is devastated by sorrow. I see a weakened woman. I look into her eyes again and this time they say, a little more tenderly, *But what is done is done. I shall not condemn you again.* And then I start to cry too. I cry because I'm happy to know I have a friend who is able to forgive.

The most surprising thing, however, is the sight of my mother without her long blond hair. What an occasion! How was Mbila able to walk the streets of Geneva without it? OK, she has still gone to the trouble of hiding her own-own hair under a little silk scarf. It isn't just her hair, though—there's no foundation, no lipstick, not even a dash of mascara. She doesn't want to make up the words in her eyes.

I finally decide to break the ice.

"You're so beautiful."

Mbila blows her nose and sniffs loudly. She doesn't reply. Maybe I said something stupid. Maybe I should have pulled some drawers over my mouth.

"Why?" my mother finally asks, hoarse. "Why did you do that to me? Why did you leave me all alone? Why didn't you think about me?"

Those are the very words I saw in her eyes a few minutes ago. I feel guilty. I feel like dropping to my knees to ask for forgiveness, but I can't find the courage to do so. I look down, and she says, "But what is done is done. I won't condemn you a second time after you've already been given so many years in prison."

Mbila doesn't stop talking. Her voice trembles. She tells me about Papusha, William's mother. She says Papusha fell into a deep depression after her son's death. She tells me that she, Mbila, almost took her own life. She tells me how those images of blood, bodies, violence—everything she saw when she came home a few minutes later—torment her in nightmares. She says she's thinking about leaving the fourth-floor flat on 39 rue de Berne, maybe even leaving Switzerland. She doesn't know if she'll go back to Cameroon or somewhere else. She talks about her fears, her black nights, her new phobias. She says she hates the color red now. She says she's on edge about everything. Everyone seems dangerous. Everyone! It affects her so much she's unable to go out and work normally in the street. She tells me about the AP girls' unfailing support. They bring her regular meals. They keep calling to ask how she is. "If it wasn't for those girls, I don't think I'd still be alive," says Mbila.

I take one of Mbila's hands. I stroke it.

"It'll be OK, Mama. I'll get out of here. I'll fight hard to help our family. I'll never abandon you. And five years in the clink isn't that bad. It's not going to stop me. It won't change my plans to help my family. I promised Uncle, remember? Help our family until the end."

When she hears that, my mother falls to pieces. I hold her hands even tighter and ask, "How is Uncle Démoney, by the way?"

"Your uncle passed away a few days ago," she whispers, hiccuping.

~

Confronted by the scourge of unregulated building in zones where construction was not permitted, the political and administrative authorities had decided to take the bull by the horns. They couldn't just let the situation deteriorate without saying a word. The assistant divisional officers, divisional officers, mayors, governors, and a few other members of parliament who had been elected with the help of stuffed ballot boxes came together to discuss this urgent matter. The newspapers backing Papa Paul talked about a working party to restore Douala's image, which had been tarnished by those people building everywhere-everywhere. At the end of their extraordinary meeting, the political and administrative authorities unanimously decided to demolish any house that didn't meet local planning regulations. Auntie Bilolo wasn't surprised, of course.

Their decision to raze the working-class Ngodi-Akwa neighborhood didn't include any plans to rehouse the people living in those poor marshlands. That's why demolition couldn't proceed peacefully. The people due to be bulldozed out of the area decided to resist. And the leader of this citizens' resistance was none other than my comrade Démoney.

Oh boy, did that piss them off! Démoney started to get right under the skin of those good political and administrative authorities who were only trying to do their job. The folk who took too many seats at the table wanted to show Papa Paul they were taking the population's concerns seriously. That's why they got cross with Comrade Démoney, who threw a spanner in the works by sabotaging their mighty work. Who on earth did this Démoney guy think he was? Of all his outspoken, dissident comrades, he was the last survivor. Despite that, instead of showing his gratitude to Papa Paul, all he did was nitpick.

Démoney had completed primary school in the 1960s and was forever bragging about it. It was one reason, if not the main reason, they'd made him a tax inspector, he said. Now that his job collecting taxes had been taken from him, followed by the very early retirement pension he'd been offered, my comrade Démoney had nothing left to lose. All he had left was his pen to write.

Every week, Uncle published highly political opinion pieces in the opposition press. They gave him a lot of space and even let him edit a weekly politics column. He took great pleasure in filling it with stinging articles and analyses, highlighting issues that kicked up a huge stir. Uncle published articles attacking the government, the political authorities, and the system. He really let rip-o! He said the system was pampered by foreign powers. He put all that stuff about the Elysée Barbie in the newspaper too.

Auntie Bilolo found out about her husband's bad habits when she went to sell her accra banana at the cement block site one day. A young laborer came up to her, smiled, and said, "Oooooo, Ma, you'd better tell Pa to take it easy-o, or it'll be the end of him-o!"

"What on earth are you talking about, son?" Auntie Bilolo asked, busy trying to sell her accra banana.

"Well, Pa is really criticizing the politicians," said the young guy. "And that's dangerous-o!"

"What? Nonsense! You must have got it wrong, asso," said Auntie.

"No, no, Ma! I haven't. And don't pretend you don't know. Everyone around here knows Uncle Démoney isn't happy with the politicians. Everyone knows he's the one writing those articles in the *Downtrodden Cameroonians* column in the opposition paper," the young laborer explained.

"What?"

"But, Ma, how on earth can you tell us you don't know a thing? Do you think we're mougou or what? You must know; you bring those papers here every day," he continued.

"Me? But I don't deliver newspapers. I just sell my accra banana. And with everything I have to do every day, how would I find time for politics? My son, you know as well as I do that politics in this country is dangerous!" Auntie exclaimed.

"Of course, Ma. That's why we're asking you to tell Pa to tone it down. He's starting to make some noise."

Auntie Bilolo pretended she still didn't understand a single thing her customers were telling her. They even went as far as asking her not to come to the site as often.

"I don't want them saying I'm against the government when I'm just minding my own business making cement blocks to send money back to my family in the village," another worker added.

"My sons!" Auntie Bilolo begged in Bassa, hoping to explain herself better. "I swear I don't have a clue what you're talking about. I'm like you. We're the ones who get up early-early when the rooster crows and go to bed late. We're the ones who eat from the sweat of our brows. We fight hard to earn our daily bread with dignity, to feed our children. We don't hurt anyone. So what makes you think that I, Ma Bilolo, or my poor husband would stick our noses into all that complicated politics business?"

"OK, Mother," another worker from the south continued. "So how do you explain the fact that Pa Démoney wrote this article in this newspaper? You're the one who served us accra banana in this newspaper yesterday. Read this page yourself, Ma; read what your husband wrote for yourself."

"Sons, my eyes have been ruined by the smoke from my wood fire. I can't read a newspaper."

"No problem, Ma."

The cement block guy cleared his throat and began to read the article in a loud, clear voice. There were a few spots of oil that made it hard to make out the words in places. He had to hold the scrap of paper away from the sun and squint hard to read each word in the column, syllable by syllable.

⌇

After almost thirty years in power, the Biya system has once again demonstrated that it excels in greed and antipathy—an open secret. This system has once again demonstrated its intellectual dishonesty and blatant lack of common sense by seeking only to enrich itself at the expense of its wretched citizens—this too is an open secret. It is no longer a surprise to anyone. What does surprise us, the downtrodden people, is the determination and intransigence with which the regime wishes to attack those who have the least, the poorest of the poor, by pushing them out of the Ngodi-Akwa marshland area.

Of course, some may be tempted to praise these efforts as an attempt to implement urban planning regulations. However, before rushing to approve such an initiative, let us stress that no human with dignity wishes to live in a place as revolting as the Ngodi-Akwa marshland. In fact, it is because our courageous full-blooded sons have lost their dignity and the ability to dream of a better future that they have left their villages in droves, abandoning their fields and their flocks, and flooded into the cities in search of a better life. It is because land and property ownership have been destroyed by corruption, tribalism, and the powerful hand of shameless politicians that several thousand citizens have been forced to take shelter in the Ngodi-Akwa slum. And, above all, it is because we, the people at the very bottom, have lost our dignity and ability to dream of a better future that we resign ourselves to living on plots of land alongside the rats and mosquitos.

Powerless, we the downtrodden, we simply repeat our favorite Cameroonian saying—how we go do?

Yes, how we go do? How we go do about our president who lives abroad and only visits the country he runs occasionally? How we go do stop him from using bulldozers to raze the only place we have to live?

Downtrodden Cameroonians, it is time we demanded our share of the unbelievable wealth with which our country overflows. What if our president was to give up a few of his luxurious trips to Europe to ensure adequate rehousing for the people in the Ngodi-Akwa marshland? What if the members of his government were to give up even a little of what they have in their foreign bank accounts? If all those corrupt politicians who pretend to listen to our demands were to give up a tiny fraction of their evil practice of embezzling public funds, the people of Ngodi-Akwa could not only be rehoused but also eat their fill. Therefore, dear comrades and downtrodden Cameroonians, let us go out into our streets in Ngodi-Akwa and make a human shield to stop the bulldozers and the corrupt powers in this country from putting us out into the street without a solution for decent alternative housing.

Auntie Bilolo had been read a summarized version to give her an idea of her husband's tirade. Dismayed, she didn't know what to say. Her head was swimming after hearing what Comrade Démoney had written in his column. She was stunned, especially since she'd always told her husband that one day they'd be moved out of the marshland where he had decided to build his hut.

The midday sun blazed hot-hot, and Auntie Bilolo ran off through the Ngodi-Akwa lanes like a madwoman. She wanted to find her husband and demand an explanation. Didn't he know it was incredibly dangerous to take up such a staunch position in a country like theirs? How could he—a man who had known the pain of Douala's ghost towns in the 1990s—think that his columns published in an opposition paper like-like that would change the country? Hadn't he seen dozens of his dissident comrades disappear? How could he dare defy Papa Paul? Did he still believe the story of David and Goliath? Auntie had so many questions. She hoped she could persuade her husband to stop writing his columns in the opposition newspaper.

As Auntie Bilolo approached her compound, she saw a crowd of gawkers camped outside. It wasn't a good sign at all. She frowned. For a moment she thought the people of the marshland had responded to Comrade Démoney's call. But the closer she got to the slum, the better she heard the wails of distress. She panicked. She dropped her platter and the last few unsold accra banana rolled off into the mud. The starving chickens flocked for a feast.

Auntie Bilolo hurtled her way through the crowd huddled around the door to her hut. She shoved people out of the way to make a path through.

"What's going on? What's going on?" she shouted, confused.

She finally reached her front door, exhausted and out of breath. She went into the house and found her son, Pitou, in tears.

"Pitou! What's wrong? Tell me, son—what happened?"

"Papa! Papa! They killed Papa!"

Auntie Bilolo headed toward her room and made the gruesome discovery: her husband's lifeless body, a bullet in the head, his ndongo ndongo hanging from his mouth.

～

Mbila can't stop crying. Neither can I. I think she regrets her inability to forgive her brother for all the pain he caused her. I'm crying because this news of my uncle's death has shattered me. It has blown away any purpose I had, any reason I had to live. Why bother fighting through another five years in prison if I have nothing left to prove, no honor to save, no one to make proud? This news is all the more upsetting because it had all been predictable and therefore avoidable. I'm crying because my beloved uncle's funeral will take place without me. I'm crying because I'll have to wait five years before I can visit the place where my uncle's body will be laid to rest.

～

Back in my cell this afternoon, after Mbila's visit, I wonder if it's still worth worrying about how to reenter the labor force and society after my time in prison. My uncle's death has taken it out of me. I feel like it's my fault. My fault because I couldn't find a quick solution to his financial woes. Maybe some financial support would have silenced him. Maybe it would have allowed him to stop criticizing those authorities. Yes, I was too young to send him mbongo, but maybe I could have persuaded Mbila to send him something from time to time. Maybe I could have persuaded Mbila to at least help Auntie . . . Maybe . . . Maybe . . .

As I lie on my bed, I see my aunt again. I picture her as a widow, dressed in white, her palm against her cheek, her eyes red with grief. I picture her alone, facing the future for her family, her children, Loudmouth Pitou . . .

I close my eyes. I'm almost asleep. But before I doze off, I make a firm commitment to help my aunt at least. I may not have managed to support my uncle, but I will make up for it with Auntie. That's what I'll do in five years' time. And hope that death does not pass again before then.

ACKNOWLEDGMENTS

The author and translator wish to thank Dominic Thomas for championing *39 rue de Berne*; Dzèkáshu MacViban for sharing his Bakwa Books expertise; Adéọlá Naomi Adérèmí, Sarah Diedro Jordão, and Florian Duijsens for their careful reading of several chapters; Dr. Ferdinand Ngale Njume for his scientific approach to linguistic queries; and Sarah Rimmington, Claire Storey, and Neus Ferrer for their invaluable feedback and support during the translation of *39 rue de Berne*.

Born in Douala in 1986, **Max Lobe** is a Swiss-Cameroonian novelist, short story writer, and poet. In 2017, he received the Ahmadou Kourouma Prize for his novel *Confidences* about the Cameroonian Independence War. Other titles include *La Promesse de Sa Phall'Excellence, A Long Way from Douala,* and *Does Snow Turn a Person White Inside.* He currently lives in Geneva, where he founded *GenevAfrica,* an association that builds bridges between Swiss and African authors.

Johanna McCalmont is a Northern Irish translator and interpreter based in Brussels, where she works from French, German, Dutch, and Italian.